Red Phoenix

Meeting My Forever

The Brothers Macallan

Meeting My Forever
The Brothers Macallan, Book 1

Cover by Diana L.
Formatted by BB Books
Phoenix symbol by Nicole Delfs

Dedication

What an incredible journey starting this new series
has been!

I fell in love with each of the men in the Macallan clan as
I began writing this first book in the series. However,
these Scottish brothers weren't the only ones to capture
my heart. I also fell for their extended family, the
animals, and the people of the town.

It was an extra-special treat as an author to visit the real
Crested Butte and meet people who call the beautiful
mountain town their real life home. Having the chance to
chat with locals, visit the areas that would be mentioned
in the book, and see the majestic peak itself added
another dimension to Lance and Avery's story.

I made it a point to visit the fire station because of Lance
Macallan's profession. It was a true honor for me to meet
with several of the firefighters there, and I want to
personally thank Veronica and Robert for taking time
out of their busy training that day to speak with me.

Of course, I had to make a special visit to the library. I
completely understand why Avery falls so hard for Old
Rock. It is an amazing library!

I must give huge thanks to my long-time editor KH
Koehler for her help, insight, and encouragement as I
navigated Lance and Avery's story in this new genre. It
was a challenge I was excited to explore, but I definitely
leaned on her experience and knowledge of me as a writer
to get through the difficult revisions.

Many thanks to Rebecca, who shared her insight and
expertise as my developmental editor. Her humor and

graciousness were appreciated, especially when time drew short.

Warm hugs to Brenda, a dear friend and fan, who helped give authentic flare to my Scottish brothers.

I deeply appreciate both Becki and Marilyn for proofing this story and working with my deadline over the holidays. Their steadfast help is priceless to me!

Special thanks to Julia. I will never forget the night by the fire when she helped me come up with the perfect name for my boys.

To my marketing team, Jon and Ben, whose help and dedication have been invaluable. I could not have concentrated on writing Lance and Avery's story without their help behind the scenes. Their selfless support and belief in this series spurs me on.

To MrRed, only you know how crazy it really got. I have never worked so long or hard on a book. Through it all, you encouraged and supported my writing in every possible way—from the trip to Crested Butte to decorating the Christmas tree and putting it away when I ran out of time. I joyfully transferred all that love you showered on me into this book. Thank you for loving me so well!

To all my readers, new and old, thank you for supporting me as an author and for falling in love with Lance, Avery, and Moonbeam. I truly can't express how much you mean to me.

You bring my muses to life!

Love,

~Red

Friends of Red Phoenix - Group
facebook.com/groups/539875076052037

SIGN UP FOR MY NEWSLETTER
HERE FOR THE LATEST RED
PHOENIX UPDATES

FOLLOW ME ON INSTAGRAM
INSTAGRAM.COM/REDPHOENIXAUTHOR

SALES, GIVEAWAYS, NEW
RELEASES, PREORDER LINKS, AND
MORE!

SIGN UP HERE
REDPHOENIXAUTHOR.COM/NEWSLETTER-
SIGNUP

CONTENTS

New Beginnings

Avery

There is only one thing I fear more than clowns or calling customer service.

Glancing anxiously at the long line of cars behind me, I slow down to navigate the steep bend of the switchback as I drive up the tall mountain peak.

Reaching for another piece of chewing gum, I pop it in my mouth, adding to the growing wad already in there. I've read chewing gum helps with anxiety, and I need all the help I can get right now.

As soon as I pass the sign for a scenic overlook, I pull off to let the other cars pass. However, I am not about to get out of my car to "enjoy the view," because I want to avoid it at all costs. Instead, I force myself to let go of the steering wheel I've been clutching for the last hour and take several deep breaths to calm myself.

I've spent weeks preparing myself for this drive by reading a ton of books on acrophobia, the irrational fear of heights. I know that my racing heart and sweaty palms are a natural response. Closing my eyes, I repeat, "I am relaxed and in control. My fear of heights does not control me."

For an extra boost of confidence, I open my glove box and pull out the small vial of essential oils I prepared for this trip. I reapply a small amount to my wrists and the back of my neck, breathing in the scent. The earthy smell mixed with lemon helps to ground me even as I continue repeating my mantra.

With renewed confidence flowing through my veins, I start up my old metallic blue VW that I lovingly call Ladybug and continue my trek up the mountain to the small town of Crested Butte.

Being a girl from Kansas, I've never appreciated how frighteningly tall the Rockies are. Most of Kansas is as flat as a dinner plate. I glance back at the stack of self-help books stuffed in the backseat and smile at them with a sense of gratitude.

I believe to the core of my being that knowledge is power.

Pulling up to the old mountain lodge motel a few hours later, I let out a huge sigh of relief feeling grateful to still be alive. Despite all my preparations for the trip, my nerves are shattered after driving over the high mountain roads.

Sitting in a daze, I stare out the bug-stained windshield, blinking slowly as I watch the "Punny Peaks" motel sign swing gently in the breeze and think, *What an odd name for the place.*

I wasn't prepared for the state of the old mountain

lodge. It looks far more rustic than the pictures on their website. Judging by the weathered wood on the buildings, these cabins look like they were built in the 1800s.

Uncertainty grips my heart, wondering what I've gotten myself into. But I can't afford to second guess this trip, so I get out of my car and take a moment to stretch my legs. Crested Butte sits in the middle of a prehistorically dug-out bowl formation, surrounded on three sides by the soaring Rocky Mountain range. Gazing up at the tall mountain peaks towering over the small town, my heart starts to race again just thinking about the perilous drive.

I pat Ladybug gratefully and mutter, "We're sure not in Kansas anymore."

Sucking in a deep breath to calm myself, I smile unexpectedly and then snort. *The air really does smell fresh up here…*

The soothing sound of trickling water filters through my brain as my anxiety lessens, drawing my attention away from the lodge and to the river flowing beside it. This river was the main reason I picked this particular establishment over the other hotels nearby.

My gaze follows the string of identical miniature log cabins following the river's edge. I smile, wondering which one of them will be my "home away from home" for the next two weeks.

It's crazy to think that the next fourteen days will determine my future. The only reason I made this long trek is to decide if I can handle living in a community this tiny. I have to be certain before I even think of signing the two-year-long contract I've been offered as a librarian in this small town.

Glancing back up at the mountain peaks, I let out a sigh of trepidation. This is so *not* what I planned for my life.

I've always assumed I would stay in Wichita where I grew up and live close to my family. I dreamed of raising a family there and having my parents and brother be a part of my children's everyday lives.

In a world of constant uncertainty, my family has always been my rock and the only thing that ever really mattered to me.

As I stare up at the towering mountain peak called Crested Butte, I'm overcome by how completely alone and out of my element I feel. How can it be that I've only just gotten here and I'm already homesick?

Hearing a soft mewing at my feet, I glance down to see a scrawny white kitten covered in a heavy dusting of red dirt. She boldly rubs her dirty cheek against my leg as if claiming me for her own.

But the moment I bend down to pet her, she hisses in fear and jumps away.

Smiling at her tenderly, I drop to one knee and hold out my hand to her, cooing in a soft voice, "It's okay, sweetie."

The timid kitten stares at me with wide eyes, and I become completely smitten when I notice that one eye is bright blue while the other is a beautiful emerald green.

"Aren't you the cutest thing ever?"

The little furball doesn't react to my voice but continues to gaze at me with those stunning eyes. I hold my breath when she starts to walk back toward me.

Afraid of startling her again, I remain completely still. However, I can't stop grinning when I feel her soft fur brush against my fingertips. After several swipes of her cheek against my hand, the kitten allows me to pet her. The moment I do, I hear the sweet sound of a loud purr erupt from her tiny body.

The little creature has no idea how much I *needed* this simple contact…

I've felt lost ever since I got the proverbial "pink slip" letting me know that my position as school librarian had been terminated. It still breaks my heart, thinking about it.

I never imagined there would come a day when the position of school librarian ended up on the chopping block due to budget cuts. It still doesn't seem real to me.

In the two years I've worked at Bently Elementary, I've strived to create a program to engage readers and non-readers alike. It's my passion because I know the transformative power of books. So, I made it my personal mission to introduce every child to the magic and wonder of reading a new book. Although I appreciate that every subject the students learn in their classes is important, I also know a love of reading will impact their lives for a lifetime.

Heck, some of my best friends reside between the pages of my favorite books, and they are as real to me as the people I know!

My principal was impressed with the success of my program and praised me in front of the entire staff, which is why, when the ax fell, it came as such a shock.

My bottom lip trembles when I think about all those

sweet faces smiling up at me as I read some of my favorite books to them during story time. It breaks my heart wondering what's going to happen to my students now that they will no longer have the joy of checking out new books every week.

I swipe away the tears in my eyes. I realize how deeply I am going to miss being a part of their lives this year.

Standing up, I smile gratefully at the kitten. "At least I've made one friend here."

The little fluffball suddenly turns away from me and crouches down low, looking as if she's ready to pounce.

"I stand corrected..." I chuckle to myself when she darts off in a cloud of red dust, completely forgetting I exist as she bounds off to chase some unseen creature.

I rub off the dust on my pants and head to the motel office, determined to make the most of the two weeks ahead.

As I walk up to the door, I read a hand-painted sign hanging there:

Bear Feet Welcome

I stare at the bear paw print on the sign and shake my head, amused by the silly pun. Before I open the door, I spit out the wad of gum I've been chewing for hours in the metal trash can on the porch. I'm startled by the sound of an old-fashioned bell ringing loudly just above my head when I enter, and look up at it in surprise.

Talk about ancient technology...

It feels like I'm walking back in time as I glance

around the small lobby at the hand-carved mid-century bench against the wall and an old grandfather clock in the corner.

From somewhere in the back, I hear a woman with a Scottish accent call out, "I'll be with you in a minute, dearie."

I shrug as I walk up to the front desk to wait. On the counter, I see another painted sign that reads:

Welcome to Punny Peaks,
We're bear-y glad to see you!

I smirk, finally understanding the meaning behind the motel's odd choice of name. The owner must be a serious admirer of terrible puns.

I turn my head when an older woman flounces out of the back and walks over to the counter. Her gray hair is done up in a braided knot and she has a tiny cluster of pink flowers tucked in it.

The room instantly fills with positive energy. I love it when I notice that her long, plaid skirt seems to dance with each step she takes. In her charming Scottish accent, she says, "You must be Miss Snow."

Surprised to hear her call me by name, I crinkle my brows and ask, "How could you tell?"

"I've been looking forward to meeting our new librarian."

I hold my hand up and politely correct her. "Nothing's been decided yet."

She nods, apologizing with a twinkle in her eye, "That's right, my mistake." Taking a key from the row of hooks behind her, she places it on the counter with a warm smile. "You will be in Cabin 12 for the duration of your stay."

She glances at the large reservation book on the counter. "I see you've reserved it for two weeks, is that correct?"

The door opens behind me and the bell rings again, announcing a new visitor. I glance back and my breath catches the moment I see a good-looking man with a trimmed beard walk into the motel lobby. I'm instantly drawn to his unusual eyes. They are crystal green and remind me of seafoam.

When I meet his even gaze, I momentarily go mute and my heart skips a beat.

"Is that a yes, Miss Snow?" the lady asks.

"No…" I blurt, then laugh at myself and turn back to her. "I'm sorry. I meant to say yes. I'll be here for two full weeks."

"Excellent. Would you like me to use the credit card on file?"

I simply nod, a bundle of nervous excitement knowing there is a hunk of a man standing beside me.

The woman at the counter smiles at me and introduces herself. "I'm Clara, by the way."

Before I have a chance to reply, my stomach lets out an embarrassingly loud growl. I clutch my torso, trying desperately to silence it, but the sound grows louder and is impossible to ignore.

Mortified, I stand there wishing the ground would open up and swallow me whole.

Without missing a beat, Clara winks at me. "I have a

gut feeling you're hungry, Miss Snow."

As if on cue, my stomach growls again. Rather than ignore it, I embrace the ridiculousness of the moment with a laugh. Following her lead, I respond, "My gut tells me you're right."

Placing the key in my palm, she squeezes my hand warmly. "Let's skip introductions for now so you can get yourself something to eat after the long trip. Lucky for you, there's a diner just up the road. Be sure to tell Bram I sent you."

Clara then turns to the man with the sexy beard. "Would you please escort Miss Snow to her cabin?"

He glances at me, immediately winning me over with his charming grin. "Of course, Granny."

Suddenly realizing the two are related, I find it adorable that he addresses her as "granny".

When he proceeds to walk to the door and open it for me, I almost swoon inside.

Determined to play it cool, I thank him as I head out into the parking lot, but as I pass next to him, my stomach growls again.

I catch the slightest smile on his lips, and a blush suddenly colors my cheeks.

Clara calls out from the counter, "Trust me, Miss Snow. You are going to love it here in Crested Butte."

The moment I hear her words, I feel a fluttering in my stomach that has nothing to do with hunger pains or the handsome man beside me. It's the type of feeling I get when something resonates in my soul.

I stop and look back at Clara, pausing for a moment. I get the distinct impression that this vivacious woman is privy to something I'm not.

I continue out the door, wondering what the next two weeks have in store for me.

Destiny Calls

Lance

After shutting the office door, and turning to our new guest, I keep my smile to myself as I look at the shapely lass with the crown of strawberry blonde curls. Not only does Miss Snow have the most enticing pale blue eyes I've ever seen, but her pert little nose is covered in a sprinkling of freckles.

Freckles happen to be a weakness of mine…

"Follow me," I direct her, leading Miss Snow down the row of cabins. She may not be aware of it, but the entire town has been waiting for her to visit. Crested Butte has been without a full-time librarian for far too long.

The town was hit hard when our longtime librarian, Effie Morris, passed away unexpectedly. Her death left a hole in the community we have yet to fill. Unfortunately, due to the small size and isolated nature of Crested Butte, the board has so far been unable to contract a qualified candidate willing to take her place.

Miss Snow is not the first candidate to show interest, but the town remains hopeful she'll be the last.

As we walk past the long line of miniature cabins, I hear the amusement in her voice as Miss Snow reads the name of each sign on the door. "Canoe Believe It? Lazy Daze…Bear Necessities…" She snickers softly when she reads, "The S'more the Merrier."

When my granny took over the lodge, she had way too much fun adding her unique brand of humor to the property by naming all of the cabins. I know my gran will be tickled when I tell her about Miss Snow's response.

I take her to the very last cabin at the end, which is my grandmother's personal favorite. "Cabin Number 12, Miss Snow."

She laughs when she reads the name out loud: "The Last Resort." She looks up at me with a delighted expression. "What a perfect name!"

Charmed by her nerdy enthusiasm, I'm about to reply when our eyes meet and I find myself momentarily speechless, suddenly lost in those beautiful eyes.

She suddenly thrusts out her hand and says with a shy smile, "You can call me Avery."

The moment I take her hand, I'm startled by the natural chemistry that flows between us. Normally a smooth talker, I struggle to find my voice when I answer her, "I'm Lance."

Humorously, her stomach growls again—for an incredibly long time. I act as if I don't hear it and point to the road. "The diner is a quick walk if you follow this road." I add with a wink, "However, a car would be faster, in case you're in a hurry."

She grins, pretending neither of us can hear her growling stomach. "You know a walk actually sounds lovely."

I find it hard not to laugh when it's obvious how hungry the woman is. However, I admire her spunk. "If you need anything, feel free to come by the office. There is someone on call until eight each evening."

"I'll keep that in mind," she says hurriedly.

I notice her fingers twitching as she fights not to clutch her stomach. Taking mercy on the poor woman, I turn to leave. "It was a pleasure to meet you…Avery."

"Bye!" she calls after me.

I can hear her struggling with the key as she races to unlock the door before her stomach growls again. I chuckle to myself as I walk away, realizing this moment will be forever stuck in my mind whenever I think about her.

Later that night, I find myself smiling as I lay in bed. I genuinely hope Avery puts down roots in Crested Butte. Although I seldom read books myself, I understand the importance of the library in our town. It's not only a place of learning, but our community hub. The fact that Avery is young like me would help ensure we have a librarian for a long time and bring stability to the community in the years to come.

But I realize my interest in her isn't tied to the library, but our obvious chemistry. The fact is I've never been attracted to bookish types before, but Avery is different.

Turning off the light, I settle in my bed knowing it's going to be a long day tomorrow. But, for the first time in a long time, I fall asleep with a smile on my face.

Hours later, I wake up in a sweat, my heart pounding hard in my chest. Gasping for air, I struggle to recover from the nightmare.

I close my eyes tight, forcing myself to take several deep breaths to calm myself while repeating, "It's only a dream…it's only a dream…"

Ever since I was a wee bairn, I've suffered from the same damn nightmare. It always begins with a house on fire and a mother begging for someone to save her child. Although the dream has haunted me for years, it's gotten much worse of late.

Unfortunately, I know the source of my nightly terrors.

I hate knowing that my mother died saving me in a fire when I was two. From what my brothers have shared, our mother was funny and kind—and incredibly brave. Hell, I literally wouldn't be here today if it hadn't been for her courage.

Even though I've suffered from the same nightmare for years, I'm no coward. My father has said that even as a child, I told everyone I was going to be a fireman when I grew up.

Truth be told, I think I've always had a "hero complex." I'm proud of being a firefighter. The job is vital to the community and incredibly fulfilling, as well as being irresistible to the ladies. I've never once regretted my choice of profession.

The moment I hear the sound of heavy boots moving about in the kitchen below, I feel a sense of peace wash over me. I glance at the clock and realize my dad must be starting his day earlier than usual.

Rather than stay in bed and stare at the ceiling in the dark, I throw off my blankets. I am immediately blasted by the frigid mountain air when it hits my naked body.

Quickly donning my clothes, I leave the bedroom and head downstairs. When I enter the kitchen, my father turns toward me and our eyes meet.

He immediately frowns in concern. "That dream again?"

I simply nod as I open the cupboard to get out another mug.

My dad is unaware of the fact that he subconsciously places his hand over his heart whenever I mention the dream. I'm certain it is a constant reminder of everything he's lost, and I can't help but feel guilty.

Turning away from me, he stares out the window into the inky blackness of the pre-dawn morning for several minutes before breaking his silence. "Lance, I could use some help with the back fence before you head over to the lodge today."

I set my mug on the counter and walk over to stand with him. I feel a deep sense of loyalty to my father and would do anything he asked. "Sure thing, Da. I'll let Granny know I'll be late coming in today."

He only grunts in response.

I've learned over the years not to take it personally

whenever my father gets quiet like this. It means he is lost in his own thoughts, tuning out everything and everyone around him.

Noticing the kettle steaming on the stovetop, I leave him and make the tea.

"Nothing like a cuppa," he states gratefully when I hand him a mug with a black tea teabag in it and we move to the kitchen table.

"Aye," I agree, taking a long sip, savoring the strong flavor of builder's tea. I absentmindedly stroke my beard as I sit beside him, still fighting off the remnants of my nightmare.

The two of us drink our tea together in silence.

My father suddenly sets his mug down and tells me, "Lance, I noticed Maisie was missing last night after I went to feed her. I didn't realize until then that the fence is down."

I look at him in alarm. "Did she escape?"

"Aye, I got on the tractor and headed out through the opening to chase her down."

I furrow my brow. "Were you able to find her?"

In his thick Scottish accent, he replies, "Aye, son…I *trac*-tor down."

I am completely unprepared for his humorous reply because of his matter-of-fact delivery, and initially miss his play on words. As I take another sip from my mug, I glance at him.

The moment I catch the sly smile playing on his lips, I almost spit out my tea as I burst out laughing.

My granny is the one famous for her puns, so I didn't even see that one coming. Shaking my head in disbelief, I mutter, "And here I was wondering why the heck you needed the tractor to find our cow…" Nudging him in the ribs, I add, "You had to make a mighty big stretch there to make that punchline work."

He chuckles. "Aye, that I did. But it was worth it to hear you laugh."

I know my father worries about me. He has always been a tad overprotective of me. Having grown up without my mother, he's had to play both roles in my life.

Taking another sip from my mug, I ask him, "Other than 'mending the fence', what else have you got planned for the day?"

"Same as any other day, laddie."

I know that means he's going to feed the animals, clean out the stalls, milk the cows, and collect all the eggs the hens laid overnight.

"If the weather holds this afternoon, I plan to start tilling the back forty so I can plant the rye."

I look at him with a sense of admiration. "You never slow down, do you?"

"Nae….no reason to. If I have time to sit, I've got time to work on something worth doing."

"But everyone needs a break, Da," I remind him, concerned that he's overdoing it. "Ever think of taking a vacation?"

The kitchen fills with his laughter. "The whole time on vacation, I'd be thinking about all of the things waiting for me back home." He raises his eyebrows. "I wouldn't consider that relaxing at all."

"You're one in a million," I concede, realizing the

man will never slow down no matter what I say. In honor of that, I clink my mug against his.

He looks at me thoughtfully. "When you concentrate on what's most important to you, you don't need a break from it." Taking a long draught of tea, he asks. "So, how've things been at the lodge lately?"

"Granny seems to be handling things well enough. Now that tourist season in winding down, the workload has lessened considerably."

He raises an eyebrow. "I suspect that has you feeling antsy again, eh?"

I nod. I've worked at my grandmother's lodge ever since I was sixteen. Even after landing my job as a fireman, I've continued to help her out on my days off. Downtime makes me uneasy.

"This time of year is always a challenge for me," I admit to him, shrugging. "I guess I take after you. I always need to be busy doing something or I go stir-crazy."

He stares at me for several moments before asking, "If you only had one year to live, what would you want to accomplish with it?"

I snort in amusement. "What kind of question is that?"

"I want you to think about it, Lance. If you knew you only had a year left, how would you leave your mark on the world?"

I sit back in my chair. "That's a loaded question."

"It is, but what comes to mind?" he presses.

I mull it over as I sip my tea, but I find I'm drawing a blank and chuckle uncomfortably. "I honestly have no idea."

"Well, I'd like you to think seriously on it, son. The moment you discover what it is, I guarantee you won't be plagued with those antsy feelings anymore." Downing the last of his mug, he gets up from the table. "Well, I'd better get started…'"

I smirk. "So, does the fence really need to be repaired?"

"Aye, it does," he answers with a low chuckle. "That part of the story was true."

I stand up and grab my jacket off the hook. "How about I clean out the stalls while you milk the cows? That'll leave you plenty of time to till the back forty after we've mended the fence."

"What about your shift at the lodge?" he asks in concern.

"I plan to call Granny to let her know I'll be late. I'm sure it won't be a problem."

"I appreciate the help, son." My father claps me firmly on the shoulder and chuckles. "Lord only knows what mischief Maisey might have gotten into last night if I hadn't found her when I did."

After fixing the fence, I return to the house for a quick shower before heading to Punny Peaks.

Wiping the steamy condensation from the bathroom mirror, I take a long, hard look at myself, thinking back on the conversation I had with my father. Still unable to answer his question, I feel that antsy feeling bubbling up to the surface again.

I'm in desperate need of a change.

Feeling an odd sense of urgency, I pull open the drawer and pick up my electric razor. With each pass through my beard, I feel more exposed—but a wee bit freer. Once the deed is done, I graze my hand over my smooth jaw.

It has been a long time since I've seen this face…

Before I head to the motel, I grab leftovers from the fridge so I can eat them on the drive. I turn the ignition, absently glancing in the rearview mirror. I'm momentarily caught off guard when I catch a glimpse of my clean-shaven face.

I'm curious about how people will react when they see me.

The Macallan men are famous for their beards. In a community as small as ours, I suspect my bare face is going to start some tongues wagging.

A Mew for Help

Avery

After a moment of fumbling with the metal key, it finally slips into the lock. But I struggle to get the darn thing to turn and grumble irritably, "Who the heck uses metal keys in this modern age?"

I find the name "The Last Resort" perfect because it is not only an appropriate pun for the last cabin on the property, but it perfectly sums up my life right now.

I have to give the door a hard push with my shoulder. Once I finally make it inside the cabin, my aggravation instantly evaporates. While booking my stay, I noticed how painfully outdated their website was. The site only had a few pictures highlighting the river and iconic mountain peaks rather than of the motel itself. I naturally assumed the cabins must be pretty basic. That was only further confirmed after seeing the motel office in person.

I certainly wasn't expecting to see a four-poster pine

bed covered in a beautiful handmade quilt when I entered. Adding to the cabin's charm, I note that the curtains on the windows match the floral designs found in the quilt. The quaint little cabin is set up like an efficiency apartment. It has everything I need, including an enclosed toilet and an open tub hidden behind a flowery shower curtain. To top it off, there's even a full kitchenette in the corner, complete with a miniature stove, dishwasher, and fridge. However, it only takes a split second for me to realize there is no microwave.

Damn, I never even thought to ask…

This unexpected surprise is going to be a serious problem for me. Among my teacher friends, I'm affectionately known as "Avery Burnsalot".

Sadly, just thinking about food causes my poor stomach to growl painfully. Still interested in walking to the diner so I can get a lay of the land, I lock the cabin door and start down the gravel road. It's bordered on both sides by grassy fields, with the impressive mountain the town is named for towering in the distance.

As I stare at the peak, a shiver runs down my spine. I imagine what the view must be like at the top.

It must be terrifying!

My stomach growls again and I pick up my pace as soon as I see the sign *Annie's Home Cookin'* ahead. Although the diner is outside of town, the small parking lot looks packed. If the locals come here, then Annie must know how to cook.

The moment I step inside the diner, my senses are greeted by the delicious aromas of home cooking. Glancing around the bustling diner, I quickly realize there's not a table to be had.

In fact, the only seat left is an empty stool at the counter. I sigh nervously. Not only can everyone watch me while I eat, but it forces me to interact with the strangers sitting next to me. Thankfully, I have a solution for that. I pat my purse as I make my way to the stool, safe in the knowledge that I have a book nestled inside waiting to be read.

I plop myself down on the stool and immediately grab a small menu tucked in the condiment rack. As I glance over it, I casually listen to the animated chatter around me, hoping against hope that my stomach stays quiet despite the yummy smells floating out of the kitchen.

The tiny menu has the traditional favorites you would expect, like chicken fried steak, meatloaf, and onion rings. However, I notice there are a few things I have never heard of, such as Cock-a-leekie soup, Clapshot, and Cranachan.

I take another quick glance around the diner and am disappointed to see only one waitress manning all of the tables. I groan inside, worried I'm in for a terribly long wait.

To my relief, a tall man with an impressive beard appears from the back kitchen carrying a large plate. He slides it across the counter to the older gentleman sitting next to me. "There you go, Russ."

"Thank you, Bram," the man answers, grabbing his fork and knife. "I'm so hungry, I could eat a horse."

My ears perk up the moment I hear that unusual name Clara mentioned. I call out to the man before he has a chance to return to the kitchen. "Hi, Bram!"

The guy turns and stares at me for a long moment, looking confused. "Do we know each other?"

As I'm about to answer, our eyes meet and my jaw drops when I see he has the exact same crystal blue eyes as Clara.

Is it possible they're related?

When I fail to answer him quickly enough, Bram turns and heads back into the kitchen, muttering to me, "I'm swamped right now. I'll be back when you're ready to order."

"Clara sent me!" I cry over the din of chatter and silverware scraping on plates. At this point, I'm too hungry to care about embarrassing myself in front of everyone.

Bram turns around slowly and grins. "So, you've met my gran, have you?"

I immediately return his easy smile. "Yes! I just came from the Punny Peaks motel."

"Ah…then you must be the librarian everyone's been talking about."

I'm startled to hear that the town is talking about me, but I'm too hungry to care right now, and plead, "Can I get a grilled cheese?"

He looks surprised by the order and asks, "Are you sure that's all you want?"

My stomach grumbles, and I nod vigorously. "I know how swamped you are, but is there any possible way you could ask the chef to make it quick?" I clutch my abdomen, confessing, "I'm afraid my stomach is about to break out in a concert if I don't eat soon."

"A concert, huh? That sounds entertaining." When I open my mouth to protest, he smirks. "It shouldn't be a problem."

"Thank you!" I gush, watching with profound relief as he disappears back into the kitchen.

Pulling my book out of my purse, I open it up to read. However, being as hungry as I am, I struggle to concentrate on the words and find myself staring at my book while I listen to the conversations all around me.

I was right about this place being a local hangout because the main topic of conversation is centered on a cow getting loose and eating some neighbor's giant pumpkin that was set to break a record at the town's fall festival.

Apparently, it is quite the scandal!

"One grilled cheese coming up," Bram announces a few minutes later, sliding the plate to me. I stare down at the blessed sandwich, licking my lips in anticipation. To my surprise, he also places a huge cinnamon roll beside it. "Compliments of my gran."

"Oh, my!" My mouth waters when I catch a whiff of the sweet cinnamon and yeasty dough.

"Feel free to eat dessert first. I promise I won't tell anyone," he tells me with a wink before heading back into the kitchen.

Taking Bram up on his suggestion, I pick up the warm cinnamon roll and take a giant bite. I close my eyes as I moan in decadent pleasure. The cinnamon roll is light and fluffy, with the perfect ratio of cinnamon and sugar. Before I know it, I've eaten the whole thing.

Still ravenous, I lick my fingers before diving into the

grilled cheese. I enjoy the gooey meld of cheeses and the satisfying crunch of impeccably grilled bread. With my stomach finally content, I smile in satisfaction, riding the visceral high that only a well-cooked meal provides.

When Bram burst out of the kitchen again, I'm bursting with praise. "Seriously, that is the best cinnamon roll on the planet! And the grilled cheese…." I give him a chef's kiss. "…pure perfection."

He nods, obviously pleased to hear it.

"Would it be possible for me to thank Annie personally?" I ask him hopefully.

Bram's grin transforms into a scowl. "No!"

Without another word, he turns back around, pushing the kitchen door open with such force that it swings back and forth violently after he's gone.

Confused by his reaction, I suddenly become acutely aware that the entire restaurant is eerily silent. Glancing around, I'm a little surprised to find that everyone is staring at me, including a little boy sitting at the table far in the corner.

Russ, the man sitting next to me, leans over and says in a hushed voice, "Annie's dead. Bram built this diner to honor her."

I feel absolutely horrible as I glance back at the kitchen door slowly swinging back and forth. Muttering softly more to myself than to him, I say, "That's so sad…"

Russ gives me an awkward pat on the back. "It's okay, honey. You didn't know. You're an out-of-townie."

Unwilling to cause Bram any further discomfort, I

grab my purse and place a wad of cash on the counter before quickly rushing out of the diner.

Keeping my head down, I hoof it back to the motel, trying hard not to think about the pained look on Bram's face. There's no way I could have known, but I deeply regret my insistence that he retrieve Annie for me.

The fact that he runs the diner in honor of her has to be one of the sweetest things I've ever heard. And it's obvious by his reaction just how much Bram loved her.

Wouldn't it be amazing to experience that kind of love?

I've never experienced love like that in real life, although I've read plenty about it in books. My parents are the best of friends, but as a couple, they seriously lack in the romance department. They prefer to be family-focused instead.

While I appreciate their commitment to my brother and me, I've always dreamed of finding someone who is not only my friend but my amorous lover as well.

Is it wrong to want both?

After my harrowing drive yesterday, and a rough night of sleep, I decide to pamper myself by spending the morning in bed reading Colleen Hoover's latest release. I get so caught up in the story that I finish the entire thing by noon. After being put through the wringer emotionally, I set the book down with tears in my eyes.

Just like the heroine, I have a tendency to try and see the best in people. It's led to several failed relationships that ended badly. I'd always assumed when I went to college, I would find my future husband and get married right after I graduated. When that didn't happen, I chose to focus on my career instead. I still hold out hope that I'll get married someday, but working in a school with a staff of primarily women hasn't helped my chances.

Furthering my career is the whole reason I'm visiting Crested Butte. I need to discover if I can survive living in a small mountain town for two years, far away from my family and friends.

In need of a brisk walk to embrace all the feelings that the book evoked, I head back down the dirt road again. Rather than brave another visit to the diner, I walk to a convenience store farther down and buy several grab-and-go meals to throw in my mini fridge. Although I have every intention of visiting the diner again, I'm not quite ready to deal with my faux pas from yesterday.

While on my stroll, my eyes keep being drawn to the intimidating mountain peak. I notice that Crested Butte is covered by low-hanging clouds even though it's a warm sunny day. It seems funny to me, and I take a picture of it with my phone and text it to my brother.

He immediately calls me back. "I take it from the photo you sent that you survived the drive."

"Barely!" I laugh. "These mountains are absolutely terrifying, Jake. You would *not* believe how high the drop-offs are or how freaking steep the roads get." I physically shudder as I think back on the ordeal.

"But you made it, sis, like the badass you are. So, tell me, what's Crested Butte like?"

I frown, my emotions still in a jumble. Looking at

the ragged peaks surrounding the area, I answer, "It's pretty, I guess…if you like grossly tall mountains."

He snorts. "Give it time. I'm sure the mountains will start to grow on you."

I sigh. "I feel so out of place here, Jake. I knew this town was small, but I didn't anticipate how strange that would be. Everyone seems to know who I am…which is unnerving."

"I bet it's impossible to be a wallflower in a place that small."

"No kidding! I *need* the escape of being able to anonymously sit at a coffee shop while I read a book. I never appreciated the privacy a big city gives you…until now."

"Huh… never thought about it that way before, but you're right."

Hearing his voice makes me homesick again. Tears prick my eyes when I tell him, "I miss you, little brother."

"Miss you, too." He pauses for a moment. "Look, I know this is hard for you, Avery. But remember why you're there. You love being a librarian. I'm proud of you for pursuing your dream…we all are."

"Thanks," I reply half-heartedly.

"Being a librarian is all you've ever talked about growing up. You're passionate about sharing your favorite books, and you excel at—"

My phone beeps three times, alerting me that my call has been dropped. Needing to hear his pep talk, I try to call him back several times, but it won't go through. Looking at the bars on my phone, I realize the reception is practically nonexistent here and stomp my foot in frustration.

In the silence that follows, I hear plaintive cries that I recognize as faint mewing. Slipping my phone back into my purse, I pinpoint where it's coming from and leave the gravel road, walking to a nearby ditch.

The panicked meows grow louder as I approach a metal drainpipe with a thin line of water trickling out from it. It's large enough that a small person could crawl through it with no issues. I call out to the cat, but the desperate mewing doesn't stop. Growing concerned that the poor animal might be hurt, I get down on my hands and knees, doing my best to not get wet as I peer into the dark pipe.

The meows instantly grow more desperate, but I can't make out a darn thing in there. Pulling out my phone again, I turn on the flashlight and spot the glint of metal grating tangled with debris several feet in front of me. And then I see what I'm looking for…two tiny luminous pinpoints of light staring back at me from behind the tangled mess blocking her escape.

I wonder if it's the tiny kitten I met at the lodge. "Come here, sweetie," I call to her as I reach out my hand, but the kitten is entangled by the debris and too far in for me to grab her.

"How the heck did you get yourself trapped in here?" I ask aloud, repositioning myself and straining harder in my attempt to reach her. This time, I lose my balance and my feet land in the water. "Crap!"

I pull back from the pipe, lamenting that my new shoes are now wet.

The little kitten's mews suddenly become more desperate in tone, and I grow concerned when I notice that the water is flowing faster.

"I can't reach you!" I call into the dark pipe, feeling as desperate as the kitten sounds. "You have to turn around and go back the way you came," I shout to her even though I know the kitten can't understand me.

My heart skips a beat when I realize there's only one thing I can do. Even though I hate the thought of squeezing into that dark pipe, I start taking off my shoes and laying them in the grass, along with my socks.

I lean down beside the pipe and hesitate for a moment. I *really* don't want to get my favorite shirt stained by whatever sludge is covering the interior of the pipe.

Since I'm in the middle of nowhere, I choose practicality over modesty. Glancing around to verify I am indeed alone, I quickly unbutton my blouse and slip it off my shoulders, throwing it next to my shoes. Liking my bra too much to sacrifice it, I take it off too.

Naturally, that's when I hear the rumble of a truck as it pulls up. Hastily grabbing my shirt, I use it to cover my bare chest.

To my mortification, the driver of the red truck lowers the window. Loud music bursts from the cab as the lyrics to John Denver's "Rock Mountain High" ring through the air. The driver quickly shuts it off and I hear a low masculine voice call out, "Is everything okay?"

I turn to face the man, my cheeks burning with embarrassment. However, my concern for the kitten far exceeds any self-consciousness I feel in having him catch me in a state of undress.

"No, it's not!" I cry out to him urgently. "There's a

kitten stuck behind the grating and the water is rising."

Quick as a flash, he jumps out of his vehicle and rounds the truck. I'm caught off guard the moment I realize it's the same hunk I met at the hotel—only he looks different today. Instead of a beard, his face is clean-shaven.

I didn't think it was possible, but Lance looks even sexier without the facial hair. In fact, he is looking hot with a capital "H" in those tight-fitting jeans and the thin T-shirt that shows off his muscular chest.

Despite the awkwardness of the current situation, I find myself captivated by his charming smile and those seafoam green eyes.

"You're lucky I got here when I did." Pointing to the tall mountain, he adds with urgency, "It's raining hard up on the peak and all that water is about to come rushing through this outfall."

Without missing a beat, he rips off his T-shirt, showing off his rippling muscles, and tosses it to me before he heads to the metal pipe to crawl inside. Stunned, I stand alone beside the ditch, listening to the mewing kitten while I watch Lance force his muscular body into the pipe with no regard for the water pouring out.

I can't help staring at his fine butt as I hastily put my bra back on, and slip into my blouse, fumbling with the buttons. "Can you reach her?" I call out.

His voice is muffled when he answers, "No. It's tight in here and there is a ton of debris blocking the way." He starts tossing dead branches out of the pipe as quickly as he can, trying to clear the grating.

The kitten's meows become more pitiful as the water

pours through the pipe at a much faster rate. Worried about them both, I ask nervously, "Is there anything I can do to help?"

"I've almost got her…"

The hair rises on the back of my neck when I hear a low rumbling coming from deep within the pipe.

"Hurry!" I scream.

A chill races down my spine when a torrent of water erupts from the pipe, obscuring Lance's body completely from view.

Cat-astrophe

Lance

Saving this little puffball isn't a problem for me. This isn't the first time I've rescued an animal from a hairy situation. As a firefighter in a small town with a ski resort, I've dealt with exotic birds, a rogue squirrel monkey, and even a giant iguana. However, by the time I've cleared enough of the gunk to grab the terrified kitten, I feel the pipe begin to shake violently.

I know the wall of water is coming down but there is nothing I can do to stop it.

Extending my arm as far as I can, I'm finally able to get a firm hold on the scruff of the kitten's neck and pull her to me. At the same time, I take a deep breath and hold it right before the water crashes into us. It hits with a powerful force that shoots me clear out of the pipe and sends me tumbling down the ditch.

After the initial shock subsides, I'm able to scramble up the embankment with the kitten still safe in my arms.

I hear Avery's frantic screams and turn to her. Although I'm battered, wet, and a little bruised, I smile as I hold up the drenched kitten for her to see.

As she runs to me, the relief I see shining in Avery's eyes is well-worth being a bit banged up, I decide.

"I was so frightened for you!" she cries, giving me a spontaneous hug.

It's pleasant, considering I'm still shirtless. But when Avery pulls away, I notice a blush rising to her cheeks as she openly stares at my bare chest.

Then her pale blue eyes trail up to meet mine…

The moment our eyes meet, I feel a rush in my veins. I stand there focused on her as the world falls away. Feeling the sudden urge to kiss her, I lean in just as the kitten lets out a pitiful yowl.

Kitten-blocked, I hand the frightened animal to Avery and announce in a gallant voice, "Back in your arms, safe and sound."

Avery grins at my cheesy delivery and exchanges my T-shirt for the frightened kitten. I stand back, watching as she snuggles the tiny creature against her body, murmuring softly, "You're okay, sweetie."

After slipping my shirt back on, I can only stand there wishing I could trade places with the cat. Avery looks up at me, her eyes flashing with wonder and appreciation. "That was the bravest thing I've ever seen!"

I chuckle. As a fireman, it was truly nothing. "All in a day's work."

She shakes her head vigorously. "Don't be so modest. If it hadn't been for you, I would have been crawling around in that pipe trying to rescue this little cutie when the water came down…" Her voice trails off, her eyes growing wider as she contemplates what might have happened.

Not wanting her to waste energy thinking about it, I remind her, "Your kitten is safe now. That's all that matters."

Avery shakes her head sadly as she glances at the tiny creature. "Oh, she's not mine. I have no idea who the owner is—if there is one."

Taking a closer look at the white kitten, I immediately notice that she has different colored eyes. I snap my finger behind the kitten's head and note that her ears don't even twitch. "She may have been abandoned because she's deaf."

Visibly upset, Avery asks me, "Why would you think that?"

I shrug. "The majority of white cats with two different eye colors are born deaf."

She holds up the kitten. "You poor little thing. I can't believe someone would dare abandon you because of that!"

As Avery cuddles the kitten protectively in her arms, I'm struck by how well-suited the two are for each other. "She seems to like you."

Avery frowns. "Unfortunately, I'm not in a situation where I can keep her." Looking at me with her doe-like eyes, she pleads, "Is there any way you could find her a home? Surely you know someone in this town who could use this sweet little companion."

I snort. "Sorry to disappoint you, but every person I know already has pets."

She looks visibly distraught. "Please, Lance! There must be *someone* who can take her…"

I can't stomach the thought of disappointing her. Even though I know I'm going to be kicking myself later, I make her a promise. "I'll take her in until I can find a permanent home."

Avery's eyes instantly light up. "Really? Oh, that would be wonderful!" Glancing down at the kitten, she gives the furry waif a kiss on the head before looking at me again. "I can't tell you how much this means to me!"

I feel like a superhero when I see the joy in her eyes. "After everything this animal has been through, I'd better take her to the vet to get checked out."

Pulling my phone from my wet jeans, I silently thank the Lord for waterproof phone cases. My first call is to my gran to let her know I'll be a bit longer. I then dial Mohan Das's number. The man takes care of almost all of the pets in Crested Butte—and quite a number of the livestock as well. He offers to see the kitten during his lunch break. I check the time on my phone and wonder if I can make it there in ten minutes.

The kitten digs her claws in when Avery tries to transfer her back to me. During the awkward exchange our hands touch, and I feel the spark between us again.

I'm curious if Avery feels it, too.

"I insist on paying the vet bill," she tells me.

"No need to worry about the bill. Mohan has a soft spot for strays and doesn't charge for health assessments."

"He sounds like a wonderful man." She then bats her eyes at me. "Just like you."

I wink. "You may want to rebutton your shirt, Avery. We wouldn't want the whole town talking about the two of us."

She immediately glances down at her blouse and laughs when she notices the mismatched buttonholes. "Yes…I would hate to sully your reputation on my second day here."

I smile at her, reluctant to leave. But I glance at my phone again and click my tongue. "I have to run if I'm going to make it to the vet clinic in time."

As I start toward my truck, she calls out, "I can't thank you enough for saving her, Lance."

I enjoy hearing Avery say my name. When I look back, I catch her rebuttoning her blouse as she walks to the ditch to retrieve her shoes and smile to myself. Although it was only for the briefest of moments, I glimpsed the sprinkling of freckles covering her shoulders when I saw her topless.

I shake my head with amusement. That woman is dangerous for me.

After I get back into the truck, I set the shivering kitten in the passenger seat. At that moment, she lets out a plaintive meow. Unhappy with the arrangement, she proceeds to crawl into my lap while I'm buckling up.

I decide not to fight her on it, because there's no time to spare. Quickly turning my truck around on the narrow gravel road, I glance at the rearview mirror. I see that Avery has already started walking down the road toward the motel, heading in the opposite direction. I honk twice and thrust my arm out the window to wave at her.

Glancing down at the tiny kitten purring in my lap, I'm grateful I was able to save her. The alternative is too sad to think about.

Fortunately, Avery and I crossed paths today. And, as an unexpected bonus, I now have the purrfect excuse to see her again.

Bookworms Unite

Avery

As I head back to the motel after the harrowing rescue, rain clouds on the mountain drift down to the valley. Soon enough, huge raindrops begin falling from the sky.

I sprint to my cabin to escape them, laughing wildly when I finally reach the door and shut it behind me. Still high from the adrenaline rush of the kitten rescue, I can't stop thinking about Lance. The moment when he held up the tiny kitten after saving her from her deadly fate plays over and over in my mind.

I've never met anyone like him before. He rushed in to help a practical stranger without a second thought for himself. That kind of reckless courage is foreign to me. I find it incredibly hot and a little frightening.

Realizing that I'm dripping on the cabin floor, I hurry to the bathtub and pull away the curtain of the old-fashioned clawfoot tub. I immediately turn on the water, desperate to strip off my sopping-wet clothes.

I'm surprised to find my hands shaking uncontrollably as I unbutton my blouse and can't help but wonder if it has to do with the kitten's close call or the fact that I can't stop thinking about Lance and his bare chest.

Sinking into the steaming water, I lay there daydreaming about his seafoam eyes and kissable lips. We were so close to kissing that I can almost feel his lips on mine. Although I can't deny that I'm drawn by his more physical attributes, the fact that he was kind to a woman with a growling stomach and saved a helpless kitten definitely hits my sweet spot.

Laying my head back against the curve of the tub, I close my eyes and imagine we're all alone in an open field of wildflowers.

Lance leans in for that kiss…

This time, I press my lips against his and we kiss for the first time. His low groan excites me, and I part my lips as the two of us explore each other with our tongues. I'm caught up in the taste and smell of him.

Running my hands down his bare back, I long to feel my skin against his. Slowly unbuttoning my blouse, I expose myself to his touch…

I sit up a little higher in the tub, touching myself as I give in to my delicious daydream, imagining his hands on my body.

Easing his fingers under my bra, Lance teases my nipple while we kiss. I feel my pussy respond to the simple touch. Wanting more, I remove my bra and toss it away as I smile up at him.

He cups my breasts in both hands, murmuring how

sexy I am. A skillful lover, he caresses my breasts, lightly flicking his fingers against my nipples and driving me wild.

Kissing him with abandon, I run my hands over his muscular chest and six-pack abs. Burning with desire, I go for his jeans next. Unfastening them, I slide my hand under his briefs to feel his rock-hard shaft. When I wrap my hand around its impressive girth, he growls in response.

Locked in our intimate embrace, we tease each other mercilessly until I'm wet with insatiable need. "I need you, Lance."

Bare-chested, his muscles rippling, he lays me down on the soft petals of the flowers. Quickly ridding ourselves of clothes, Lance leans over me, his naked body pressed against mine.

I look up, entranced by those seafoam eyes. I open my legs to him, my body aching to be taken…

Thoroughly lost in my sexy daydream, I'm suddenly distracted by a ping on my phone. I desperately try to ignore it, but the mood is lost.

Frustrated, I reach for a towel and wrap it around me. Tiptoeing over the wood floor, I grab my phone and check my messages. As soon as I see I have a text from the executive director in charge of the Gunnison County libraries, I get a bad feeling.

As I quickly scan the message, my heart starts to pound. I check my calendar and realize the meeting I thought was set for tomorrow is today—and I'm already late!

Can this day get any crazier?

With my panic now dialed up to ten, I rush around the cabin frantically. Throwing on the professional clothes I specifically brought for this interview, I thank my lucky stars that I'm a planner by nature. The paperwork I need for the interview is already tucked into the leather business satchel my little brother gave me for my college graduation.

Glancing in the mirror, I grimace. My hair is still a damp mess. I frantically search the cabin for my hairbrush. Dragging it through my wet hair with one hand, I brush my teeth with the other. With no time to style my hair or apply makeup, I put my hair up in a ponytail and run out the door. Tossing my satchel in the passenger seat, I start my car and peel out of the parking lot.

I groan, frustrated with myself. I can't believe I mixed up the dates. That never happens to me, and now I'm late on top of it!

I was feeling anxious about this interview already. Although Mr. Gregory assured me that the contract is mine if I decide I'm a good fit, he still insisted on meeting me personally. He sounded quite cold the last time we spoke on the phone, which does nothing for my jangling nerves right now.

Rather than feed my mounting anxiety, I repeat loudly, "I am relaxed and in control!"

Oh, how I burst out in relieved laughter a few minutes later when I pull into the parking lot. I made it a point to thoroughly study the map of downtown Crested Butte weeks before coming here. I know all the streets by name. What I failed to take into account was that the actual town is much smaller than it looks on the map.

Taking a minute to collect myself, I get out of my car with my satchel in hand. As I walk up to the two-story library, I stop for a moment. Although I've seen pictures of the historical library on the website and know the building was originally built in 1883 as a schoolhouse, seeing it in person is a completely different experience.

I must admit, I'm enchanted by the old sandstone building. It's the most charming library I've ever seen. Although I'm desperate to return to my family in Wichita, I could *almost* imagine myself working here.

As I head to the entrance, I notice a man dressed in a dark suit standing just outside. By the stern expression on his face, I assume it's Mr. Gregory.

Although I am normally shy by nature, when it comes to my profession as a librarian, I'm as confident as they come. Walking straight up to him, I hold out my hand. "I'm Avery Snow. I presume you are Mr. Gregory?"

The middle-aged gentleman nods without cracking a smile and gives me a firm handshake. Glancing at my wet hair, he states in a cool tone, "You're late."

"I know, and I'm terribly sorry. I mixed up the date of our meeting."

He frowns. "This does not bode well, Miss Snow."

"Now, now…don't go scaring her off before we've even had a chance to sit down! She's only a few minutes late."

I turn to see a cheerful woman with long gray hair stepping out of the building to meet us. She smiles when she introduces herself. "I'm Flora Elwood." Gesturing to the building, she says with reverence, "Welcome to Old

Rock."

Inviting me inside, she gives me a moment to look around. I instantly feel at home when I see the rows of bookcases, wooden tables for studying, computer stations, and several big comfy chairs.

The old library appears to have every modern convenience I'd expect to see in a public library but with the cozy vibe of a coffee shop.

"I invite you to explore every nook and cranny after our meeting, Miss Snow," she says with pride. "But, for now, please follow me upstairs. I've set out a nice tray of goodies to munch on while we chat."

I hide my trepidation as I look at the stairs. My heart is already starting to beat loudly in my chest. The wooden stairs look as old as the building itself, and I can hear the planks squeak with every step Flora takes.

Mr. Gregory gestures for me to go ahead of him. Although I'm surprised by his chivalrous gesture, I notice his expression remains cool.

Turning back to face the stairs, I remind myself that I'm safe as I grip the rail tightly. With slow, calming breaths, I start up the stairway while keeping my eyes focused on Flora's shoes. When I finally make it to the top, I let out an audible sigh of relief.

Flora misinterprets the sound, assumes I'm impressed with the layout, and turns to me. "I know! The view is amazing, isn't it?" She points to the large panoramic windows throughout the upper level that look out at the mountainous landscape.

Although I agree the scenery is stunning, seeing those tall mountains only manages to trigger my anxiety.

Turning my attention back to her, I ask in a strained voice, "Where should I sit?"

"We're meeting in the conference room." She points to the open door of a small room only a few feet away. Grateful, I happily follow her.

As I enter, I notice a small tray on the table laden with a variety of pastries. Mr. Gregory pulls out a chair for Flora first, then another for me.

Appreciating the kind gesture, I thank him as he pushes my chair in. He nods in response and sits down opposite me, reaching for a croissant off the tray.

"Remember our guest," Flora reminds him gently, then winks at me.

The man looks chagrinned and pushes the tray closer to me. "Please take whichever one you like, Miss Snow."

Although I'm not feeling hungry in the least, I take the other croissant and say with amusement, "It appears you and I have similar tastes. I wonder if that is true of books as well."

He doesn't respond, but I notice his expression softens a little. One thing I have learned as a librarian is that book lovers come from all walks of life. Although we may have completely different backgrounds, the love of books connects people like nothing else can.

As he reaches for the remaining croissant, he asks, "So, why do you want to work in Crested Butte?" He then bites into the pastry and chews it slowly, waiting for my answer.

Although I realize they may not like what I have to say, I'm truthful with them both. "Normally, I would never have considered moving away from Wichita. But, with school librarians being let go for budget reasons all over Kansas, I made the difficult decision to seek a job elsewhere so I can continue doing what I love and am trained to do."

Mr. Gregory narrows his eyes. "You do realize that living in a mountain town, our size is a marked difference from living in the suburbs of Wichita."

I hear a hint of hostility in his voice. Wanting to give myself a few moments to think about it before I respond, I pull off a piece of the flaky dough and pop it into my mouth.

Flora gives him a worried glance before speaking up, "What makes Crested Butte special is that we are more people-focused. Unlike bigger communities, folks here like to spend time outdoors. It's important to us that we balance work with our quality of life." She smiles kindly at me. "You'll find very few people in Crested Butte devoting their entire lives to work."

I'm taken aback because that certainly isn't true of the work ethic in Wichita. In my school district, it's an unspoken expectation that we devote much of our personal time to our profession. Most of us stay after work to get ready for the next day. Even summers are spent taking classes and workshops to prepare for the school year ahead. Since that is pretty much the norm, I've never given it any thought.

"What Mrs. Flora is trying to say," Mr. Gregory interjects, "is that our library focuses on the community. It's more than a knowledge resource; it is a vital part of people's lives. From fitness programs, social events, and children's activities to nutritional seminars and computer classes, it's our mission to meet the needs of our community as a whole."

I raise my eyebrows, impressed by the scope of their vision.

"You can understand why it's vital we find a dedicated librarian who stands behind that mission," Flora adds.

I nod, telling them, "The reason I've decided to stay for two weeks is to determine if I can make that commitment."

"That's wonderful to hear!" Flora says, picking up a blueberry muffin from the tray. "Wouldn't it be lovely if she attended the Fall Festival?" she tells Mr. Gregory. "It would give her a chance to mingle with the community."

Although the festival sounds charming, in a Hallmark movie sort of way, it also sounds like a commitment. So, I'm careful with my words when I tell her, "I'll certainly keep that in mind."

Mr. Gregory clears his throat, and I wonder if he can detect the uncertainty in my voice. "Unfortunately, Miss Snow, despite this town having an excellent library and the full support of the community, the last two people we hired ended up breaking their contract. I feel it is my duty to emphasize that I despise wasting *my* time and yours."

"I do understand that," I assure him. "Which is why I've come on my own dime to spend time here. I need to experience life in Crested Butte before I can make a two-year commitment." I place my hands on the table and lean forward. "One thing you should know about me is that when I commit to something, I'm all in."

Although Flora smiles, Mr. Gregory appears unfazed.

"Since we have already established your qualifications prior to this meeting, I only have a few questions."

I nod.

"Which books were your favorite as a youth, Miss Snow?"

By the tone of his voice, it sounds like a loaded question, but I'm pleased to answer him and sit back in my chair. "I've always been an eclectic reader," I explain to them both. "So, some of my favorites may come as a surprise to you."

"Go on," Mr. Gregory states.

"Naturally, I loved the mainstream classics like *Black Beauty* and *Where the Red Fern Grows*, but 1 also enjoyed science fiction and have re-read *The Martian Chronicles* and *Enders Game* many times. As far as non-fiction…I was totally broken by *Bury My Heart at Wounded Knee*."

I hold up my finger, knowing I'm missing an important one. "Oh, and I must include *Jane Eyre*. I reread that book so many times in high school that I wrote an entire research paper about the author, Charlotte Bronte."

"Eclectic, indeed…" Mr. Gregory mutters.

I'm thrilled when I see the slight tug of a smile on his lips. I grin, finally feeling the elusive bookworm connection between us.

"I only have one more question for you," he says in a serious tone. "As the librarian of Old Rock, what would be your main focus beyond the regular duties we've discussed?"

Having heard the list of activities the library already supports, I'm unsure what I can add, so I reply, "If I were librarian, since I am not familiar with the community, I would do an assessment to determine if there is a significant portion of the community whose needs have not been addressed by this library."

Mr. Gregory nods. "A fine answer."

Mrs. Flora looks pleased and asks, "Miss Snow, did you bring the information we requested?"

I immediately open my satchel and hand my paperwork to her.

Looking the forms over, she states, "Everything is in order, Mr. Gregory."

He nods to her before turning to me. "As Mrs. Elwood mentioned earlier, we expect you to spend time exploring Old Rock before you leave today. Once you've made your decision, should you wish to sign the contract, give me a call and I will have it drawn up and emailed over."

He stands up and holds out his hand to me.

While I'm shocked by the brevity of the interview, I am relieved it's over. After shaking both of their hands and thanking Flora for the pastries, I leave to face the challenge of the stairs again.

I find going downstairs even harder than going up. Thankfully, a little boy and his mother step in front of me. I happily follow behind him as he slowly makes his way down one step at a time. Rather than give in to my anxiety, I concentrate on the boy, silently praising him for his bravery.

When we finally make it to the bottom, the mother turns around and thanks me for being so patient. I smile at her, then crouch down to tell the boy, "You did such a great job going down the stairs all by yourself!" I hold up my hand and he gives me an enthusiastic high-five.

Mrs. Flora comes up behind me and whispers, "What a lovely thing to do."

Little does she know how much I meant it.

Now that I'm on the main floor again, I can let my librarian heart off the leash to run free. I start checking out every bookshelf. Running my fingers over dozens of spines, I read each title, wanting to familiarize myself with their wide selection of books.

While I'm in the graphic novels section, I notice a young man looking extremely agitated. He keeps glancing at a piece of paper he's carrying and searching the shelves.

Walking over to him, I whisper, "Can I help?"

He growls. "I've spent the last fifteen minutes trying to find this book!"

A woman looks up from the periodical section where she's reading a newspaper and glowers at the young man. "Shh…"

He glances at her, looking extremely frustrated.

Taking the paper from him, I read the title. "I bet this is in the history section."

Guiding him to it, I quickly find the title he's looking for.

"Thanks," he mumbles as he takes it from me. "I don't think I would have ever found it on my own."

"Happy to help," I assure him, feeling a surge of joy as he sits down at a table and opens the book to start taking notes.

Damn, I miss this…

Returning to the graphic novels, I overhear two women whispering heatedly behind me.

"Don't even think about it, Blair."

"Why? The man is famous and so damn talented with his hands…"

"It doesn't matter how famous or talented he is. I've heard that not one of the five Macallan brothers has ever gotten married."

"I don't care about the rumors, Lacey. Finn is different. He's a real artist, and some women can't handle his kind of intensity."

"Listen to me, Blair. The Macallan brothers are eternal bachelors—every last one of them. You're only setting yourself up for heartache."

One of the other patrons speaks up, "Date the man or don't date the man, I don't give a flying flip. But the library is for reading, not gossip."

The two women immediately get up and leave in a huff.

I shake my head after overhearing their conversation. It seems the rumor mill is alive and well in Crested Butte.

Still, I think it's probably best if I avoid anyone named Macallan while I'm here. The last thing I need is to walk into a relationship that is doomed from the start.

Moonbeam

Lance

The moment I walk into the vet's office, I notice people eyeing me strangely. When I walk up to the receptionist's desk, Sandy just smiles. "Can I help you?"

I snort, "Didn't Mohan tell you I was coming?"

She frowns for a moment before her eyes grow wide as saucers. "Lance Macallan?"

Chuckling, I ask her, "Who else?"

She blushes a deep shade of red and motions to the door. "Doc's waiting for you in room three."

When I hear people whispering excitedly behind me, I suddenly understand Sandy's odd reaction. Rubbing my hand over my smooth jaw, I smirk at her as I head to the room with the kitten resting in the crook of my elbow.

Mohan Das raises his eyebrow when I enter but says nothing as he pats the examination table. "Hurry, Lance, I haven't got much time."

"I appreciate you doing this, Doc."

"Of course," he states matter-of-factly.

After a quick examination, he says, "She looks to be seven weeks old." He glances at me with a serious expression. "I suppose you already know she's deaf?"

I nod, look down at the white furball, and ask hopefully, "I don't suppose you know anyone looking to adopt?"

"Not a soul," he laughs. "But whoever takes her needs to be informed that she'll need specialized care because of her hearing loss."

I frown. "What kind of 'specialized care?'"

"Fortunately, it's not complicated. They'll simply have to handle things a little differently with her. It goes without saying that she'll *have* to be a housecat." He pets the tiny creature, stating with admiration, "She must be a crafty little feline because I can't imagine how she managed to survive with all of the wildlife we have here."

Glancing at the clock, he says, "Other than that major restriction, she'll simply need visual cues rather than audio ones, and you'll have to approach her in a way that won't startle her."

"What do you mean by that?"

"I'd advise using vibration to alert her." He taps on the examination table to demonstrate.

I nod. "Okay, that makes sense."

"And because she can't hear, she'll be much more responsive to touch."

"Gotcha."

After giving her a series of vaccination shots, Mohan hands her back to me. "With some extra TLC over the next few days, she should settle right in. And, naturally, there is no charge for the visit."

"Thanks, Doc."

He claps me on the back. "I'm grateful you were able to rescue this little warrior, Lance. I guarantee you that somebody needs her fighting spirit in their lives."

I chuckle uncomfortably. "And I'll be hunting for that person, I assure you. But be sure to text me if you happen to find them first."

He smiles. "One more thing." Mohan lowers his voice slightly, "I've heard rumors that Killian is on the warpath after his prize-worthy pumpkin was obliterated by an unidentified bovine last night."

I look at him in surprise. "Oh, hell! We just fixed the back fence this morning."

He gives me a knowing look. "If you happen to come across a colicky cow, please inform the owner I have the cure. They have but to ask…and I'll be discreet, of course. We wouldn't want word getting out."

I grin, shaking my head. "How could you possibly know about the fence?"

"I didn't. However, I'm quite familiar with Maisey's obsession with pumpkins, as well as the proximity of your two farms. I want to prevent a war—if possible."

I chuckle. "You know, I've never understood the rivalry between my dad and Old Man Killian."

Mohan Das looks at me thoughtfully. "There are some things that only the people directly involved should share."

I frown, suspecting he has the answer I'm looking

for. "What do you know that I don't, Mohan?"

He opens the office door. "As I said, it's not for me to share."

I leave the room unsatisfied, but am deeply appreciative of his discretion when we both hear old man Killian's angry voice fill the vet clinic.

Mohan quickly guides me out the back. Before shutting the back entrance door, he examines my face closely. "Has anyone told you how much you take after your mother? I had no idea because your beard covered most of your face."

His words affect me in a way I'm not prepared for, and I am suddenly overcome with a sense of pride…and loss.

Giving me a curt smile, Mohan quickly shuts the door.

I stand there for a minute, staring at the tiny kitten in my arms. Since I'm not in the mood to deal with Killian, I hurry to my truck.

Scratching the kitten's head, I mutter, "I guess I'd better head to the pet store and get supplies until I can find you a permanent home."

Wanting to update Avery about what the vet said, I walk over to The Last Resort cabin after my shift ends at eight. Knocking lightly on the door, I wait for her to answer.

Although the cabin lights are on, I quickly realize she must have already left for the evening. Disappointed that I won't get the chance to see her again before my shift starts at the fire station tomorrow morning, I scribble a quick note on a memo pad and give her my phone number as well as a status update on the kitten.

I jam the note between the doorknob and the frame, trusting that she will find it. On my drive back to the farm in the dark, I notice the trees have started swaying back and forth.

It looks like a storm is brewing…

Once the kitten is settled in my room, I head down to the kitchen where I see my father sitting at the table with one of my older brothers, Finn.

"Well, it's good to know you're still alive," I joke when I meet Finn's eyes. "Been a while."

"I know, I know…" he chuckles. "You've probably been complaining 'Finn's chained to his sculpture again.'" He shrugs. "What can I say? I've been obsessed with this piece and lost all track of time."

"You *do* realize that's the same excuse you always give, right?" I laugh, smacking him on the shoulder as I take a seat at the table.

Finn stares at me with an odd expression. "I have to admit, I hardly recognize you, baby brother."

"You're not the only one," I reply, telling them about my recent visit to the vet clinic. Rubbing my smooth chin, I say, "It's freeing, Finn. You really ought to try it."

"Not on your life," he states unequivocally as he strokes his pointed Van Dyke beard.

"So, did you just come to gawk at my mug or is there

a reason for this illustrious visit?"

Finn snarls. "Killian came to my studio this afternoon. He's up in arms about some prize-worthy pumpkin being desecrated." He rolls his eyes in irritation. "I don't know why the hell he's bothering me about it."

My father and I share a look.

"Killian was spouting off about it at the vet clinic while I was in the back with Mohan."

Shaking his head wearily, my dad lets out a long sigh.

"What were you doing at the vet's, anyway?" Finn asks.

Knowing my brother's soft spot for animals, I realize I've been presented with a golden opportunity. "Let me show you."

I bound up the stairs to my bedroom. When I open the door, I find the kitten sitting on the windowsill, swishing her tail back and forth as she stares out at the swaying trees.

Walking over, I reach out to touch her, but pause when I remember Mohan's advice. Rather than startle the kitten who is clearly wound up, I take a few steps back and stomp my foot on the floor.

She immediately turns her head in my direction. The instant she sees me, she jumps off the windowsill and runs up to me, yowling loudly. I pick her up, declaring with excitement, "I think I've found your new home!"

Heading back to the kitchen, I hold the white furball out to him. "Meet the kitten I saved this morning."

Finn takes her from me and cradles her in his arms. "I certainly wasn't expecting this."

"She'll make a perfect addition to your home."

My brother immediately tries to hand the kitten back to me. "Nae. I already have my hands full with Scotch."

I gently push the kitten back to him. "I looked up fennec foxes while I was at work today, and they get along just fine with cats. I bet Scotch would love to have a buddy."

"Sorry, Lance. She's skittish enough as it is. I would hate to add to her stress." Finn scratches the kitten's head, telling me, "Although she's sweet, the answer is a hard no."

"You can't blame a guy for trying," I mutter, disappointed he won't be taking her home with him tonight.

"Here's a thought…" Finn replies with a smirk. "Instead of trying to pawn her off, why don't you keep her yourself?"

I feel a tightness in my chest and shake my head. Keeping her is not an option for so many reasons, and I feel the need to explain, "You know why that can't work. My schedule at the fire station would be unfair to any animal. And with her being deaf, she can't run around on the farm while I'm working those forty-eight-hour shifts."

Finn holds up the kitten and looks at her mismatched eyes. "You didn't mention she was deaf."

I shrug. "Mohan assured me it's no big deal. After she gets a little meat on her bones, she won't need extra care."

Kissing the kitten on the nose, Finn hands her to me. "I wish you luck. Such a wee thing deserves someone who will take good care of her."

The tiny kitten uses her sharp claws to climb up my arm and perches herself on my shoulder. I pat her on the head, asking my dad, "How much of the back forty did you get done today?"

"I was able to get the first ten acres because of your help with the fence."

"How is Maisey doing, by the way? Only asking because Mohan was concerned about her."

He chuckles. "She's fine. However, I did notice a distinct aroma of pumpkin while I was milking her this morning."

I chuckle at the poetic justice. "What are the chances Maisey would know to zero in on his most prized possession?"

My father shrugs, but I hear a tinge of anger in his voice when he tells us, "I'd offer to make things right, but the fool is so pigheaded and full of spite that there's absolutely no point in trying."

Although the situation is funny, my brother and I are acutely aware of the age-old rivalry between the two men. My father is a peace-loving soul, but when it comes to Old Man Killian, any decorum he might have with regard to the guy has long since flown the coop.

For some odd reason, Killian's hostility is not only targeted at my father but at me as well. It's been that way ever since I can remember, but I've never understood why. The few times I've been brave enough to ask my dad about it, he's bitten my head off and reminded me that I'm strictly forbidden from having any contact with the man or anyone in his clan.

I glance at the kitten on my shoulder and decide to try one last shot with Finn. "Are you certain you can't take her? My shift at the firehouse starts tomorrow, and I won't be back for two days."

He shakes his head. "Sorry, brother."

"I'd help you out," my father states, "but I'll be working in the field from dawn 'til dusk until it's all plowed up." He glances at the kitchen clock and stands up. "And on that note, boys, I'm headed to bed."

I watch him slowly walk up the stairs, wishing I could be around tomorrow to help him. My dad never complains, but I know he carries a ton of responsibility on his shoulders running the farm without my mother by his side.

I let out a sigh, still unsure of what to do with the cat. The kitten, who has remained on my shoulder the entire night, responds to my yawn by rubbing her cheek against my jaw.

Smiling despite myself, I mutter to Finn, "Since I can't leave her alone, that means I'll have to bring her with me to the firehouse."

"You know Fire Chief Higgins won't allow that."

"Luckily, the Chief's on vacation and it'll just be for two days so he'll never know."

My brother clicks his tongue. "Sounds like trouble, if you ask me."

I sit back in my chair. "I figure if I can't get anyone at the firehouse to take her, maybe I'll meet someone on a call who needs a kitten."

Finn gets up from the table, smirking at me. "I love your optimism, brother. But when you get your butt chewed out by Higgins, don't forget I told you so."

After seeing Finn off, I head upstairs with the kitten. Placing her on the foot of the bed, I quickly undress and turn off the light. Slipping under the cold sheets, I listen to the wind howl outside.

The tiny furball wakes up with a start and meows. Running up the length of my leg, she settles down on my chest and starts to purr. Although she's sweet, I can't allow her to stay.

As a firefighter, I never know which day may be my last. I've learned to avoid emotional attachments of any kind after watching my father struggle without my mother.

I don't want to hurt someone the way I've seen my father hurt after losing the woman he loved.

I glance out the window at the full moon shining brightly in the night sky. There is a mystic quality to it tonight because it's surrounded by a bright halo.

The old saying, "Ring around the moon means rain soon" automatically plays in my head, and I chuckle to myself.

It's odd the things that stick with you...

Although I'm normally a side sleeper, tonight I remain on my back, not wanting to disturb the tiny kitten purring on my chest. As I stare at the white puffball curled up on my chest, her name suddenly pops into my head.

Moonbeam.

Even though I can't afford this tiny complication in my life, I'm still glad she's here.

Unexpected Guest

Avery

I smile, thinking back on the interview. After spending hours acquainting myself with the library, I'm even more fascinated by this place. On my way out, I look back at the beautiful sandstone building brimming with knowledge.

In a carefree moment, I spread my arms wide and twirl as I smile up at the sky.

That's when I hear Mr. Gregory clear his throat.

I immediately stop and turn in embarrassment, realizing I had failed to notice the gentleman standing under the shade of a pine tree. Remembering one of my favorite quotes from *Jane Eyre*, I tell him, "I would always rather be happy than dignified."

He nods. "Charlotte Bronte wrote poignant words, didn't she?"

It's a magical moment when you discover you have a favorite author in common with someone. I can't stop smiling knowing that under Mr. Gregory's serious demeanor beats the heart of a true bookworm.

"Good day, Miss Snow."

"Thank you, Mr. Gregory."

After driving back to my cabin, I set my satchel down and collapse on the four-poster bed, laughing out of sheer joy. Reluctant to leave the comfortable bed, I pull out my well-worn copy of *Jane Eyre* from my stack of books on the nightstand.

It's one of my go-to books—a part of my "comfort" reading.

I became acquainted with Jane in my school library. She quickly became a dear friend when I read how she overcame her struggles at school. I admired her for never wavering from being her authentic self even in the face of extreme adversity. I rooted for Jane to succeed through impossible odds because it made me believe that I could, too.

However, what cemented her as a friend for life to me was how she remained loyal and devoted to the man she loved, despite the ways fate conspired against them.

Although I know Jane is a fictional character, she is someone I admire and continue to find inspiration from every time I read her story.

Diving right in, I get so lost in Jane's world that I don't even remember falling asleep. To be honest, that happens more times than I care to admit.

I wake up with the book still in my hands and laugh at myself. Setting it on the nightstand, I lay in bed, listening to the wind howl wildly outside.

I'm desperate to hear news about the kitten, but it's

too late to ring the front desk and see if I have any messages. As I lay in my warm bed, I'm drawn to the brightness of the moonbeams shining through the window.

Leaving the comfort of my bed, I walk to the window to gaze up at the moon. I'm surprised to see the full moon has an iridescent "fairy ring" around it. It's truly magical!

Closing my eyes as if I'd just seen a shooting star, I make a wish.

If I'm meant to stay, give me a sign tomorrow.

I wake up in the morning feeling refreshed and ready to start my day.

After my trouble with the stairs at Old Rock, I am now on a mission. I can't allow my fear of heights to control my life. Taking inspiration from Jane's tenacity, I plan to do something incredibly daring today.

Before I do, however, I head to the front desk to see if Lance is there wanting to hear news about the kitten. I notice that the air is crisp after the intense windstorm during the night, giving it an extra sweetness.

As I walk up to the office, I hear a man speaking very loudly, his words muffled by the closed door. The moment I open the door, the bell rings above my head and the heated discourse stops.

Clara and a tall man with a red face turn to look at me. I smile hesitantly, but before I can speak, the man turns back to her and pounds the desk. "I demand justice! I *know* it was your son's cow that destroyed my pumpkin. Don't you deny it!"

"Haud your wheesht!" Clara barks at him. Then she turns to me and smiles sweetly. "Is there anything I can help you with, lass?"

The angry man glares at me, his nostrils flaring.

"I…I was just wondering if Lance is here?"

She smiles when I mention his name. "Nae, it's his day off. Is there something I can help you with?"

I shake my head. Responding to the intense ire emanating from the man, I ask her, "Perhaps, you could use a hand?" I'm more than happy to phone the police for Clara's sake.

She chuckles, giving the man the side-eye. "Nae, but I appreciate the offer, lass."

The moment I turn to leave, the man starts up again. "What are you going to do about it? I demand to know!"

"Mister Killian, you will *not* speak to me in that manner, especially in front of my guests. This is a place of business. Away with ye!"

Her tone immediately silences him.

The bell rings loudly as I open the door and exit, shaking my head. I had no idea that a simple pumpkin could create this kind of drama.

Heading back to the cabin, I make a quick call to my parents. I share about the daring kitten rescue and then give them a quick update about my interview. When they ask if I'm seriously considering taking the position, I admit, "I'm hoping today will bring me some much-needed clarity."

"If you decide to stay, you know your father and I support you," my mom assures me.

My father adds, "But I'll miss you something fierce, Pumpkin."

After the heated discussion I just witnessed about the squash, I smirk when I hear his nickname for me. Still, I can sense the sadness in his voice and it pulls on my heartstrings.

The need to return home is strong.

Parking near the chairlift, I stare up at it from the safety of my car. Even though it's September, the lift is still in operation, taking hikers and cyclists up the mountain. Just watching the chairs slowly advance up the mountain starts my heart racing.

I trust I'm brave enough to meet this challenge.

I jump with a start when my phone rings. I immediately smile when I look to see who it is. "Hey, Jake-o."

"What's going on, sis? I just got off the phone with the ol' parents. Pop seems convinced you're never coming back."

I burst out in nervous laughter as I continue to watch the seats in the lift sway gently. "Well, you know Pop…he's just being overdramatic."

Jake snorts. "I figured as much but wanted to check in with you anyway."

I get out of my car and lean against it, never taking my eyes off the chairlift. "I have to admit, the interview went well, and I love the library. Cutest one I've ever seen."

"That sounds promising. But Da also mentioned something about you nearly drowning."

I roll my eyes. "I wasn't the one who almost drowned…" I proceed to tell him a more detailed version of the kitten story than I shared with my parents.

"That sounds terrifying. How is the cat doing now?"

I let out a worried sigh. "I assume she's fine. The guy who rescued her said he was taking the kitten to a vet, but I haven't heard a word since."

"Hang on."

"What?"

"Are you attracted to this guy?"

I roll my eyes, because I specifically kept my description of Lance simple with my brother for this exact reason. "Why would ask?"

"I'm picking up something weird in your voice."

I huff. "I have no idea what you are talking about."

"Sure you don't."

"I don't even know the guy."

"But you want to…" he teases.

I smirk, knowing I've been outed. "Like I said, I don't know anything about him. With my luck, he's probably engaged and about to get married."

"Or he's a serial killer who rescues kittens to win over the trust of his next victim…"

"Thanks, little brother."

"Hey, I know your taste in men."

"You're such an ass," I laugh.

"Seriously, sis. How invested are you in this guy?"

"Good grief! I told you I don't even know him."

"Fine. I'll stop giving you a hard time. So, tell me your plans today. Will you be spending the entire day holed up in your hotel room reading books, or are you going to spice things up and read outside instead?"

"Very funny. For your information, I'm currently looking at a chairlift going up a mountain that doesn't have any snow. I never even knew that was a thing."

I hear the surprise in Jake's voice when he asks, "Are you going on it?"

"Maybe."

"Wait. I'm seriously questioning if you've been abducted by aliens right now." His tone changes when he asks with concern, "What's really going on, sis?"

I pause for a moment, before letting out a ragged sigh. "Yesterday, when I was at the library, I watched a three-year-old boy walk down the stairs without any fear." Tears prick my eyes as I stare at the chairlift.

"I want to be able to do that, Jake."

After our call, I ready myself for the challenge ahead.

Feeling like a warrior preparing for battle, I rub essential oil on my wrists and neck, slipping the vial into my pocket. I then pop a piece of gum in my mouth, and then bring the whole pack "just in case".

Staring at the chairlift, I embody the fortitude of Jane Eyre as I head out to face my greatest fear. My heart beats like a hummingbird as I walk up to the terminal. The metal structure is bright red with the words "Red Lady" painted on the side.

I wait in line, watching as the people get on the lift ahead of me. Even though my body is literally shaking, I keep the little boy's courage in mind each time I advance.

But I forget to breathe as I step onto the loading area and wait for the next chair to swing around. Grabbing tightly onto the sidebar, I sit down, close my eyes, and finally let out my breath.

Behind me, I hear a commotion as one of the workers shouts, "Everyone step back and make way for the emergency responder."

Suddenly, the double-seated chair shudders as a fireman joins me on the lift and lowers the safety bar.

He turns his head, looking as surprised to see me as I am to see him.

Even though Lance is wearing dark sunglasses, I instantly recognize him. He's dressed in a firefighter uniform with a tactical bag strapped across his shoulder and a dark blue cap with the red letters.

His grin is infectious when he jokes, "You and I seem to have a knack for racing toward trouble together."

I let out a terrified squeak when the chair starts to swing as it pulls away from the ground.

Seeing my obvious distress, he chuckles lightly. "Didn't mean to scare you, Avery. But don't worry, you're safe with me."

Strangled laughter escapes my lips as I clutch the bar in quiet desperation and nervously chew my gum.

I am relaxed and in control, I whimper in my head.

As the lift rises toward the mountain ahead, I distract myself by looking at Lance and not at the ground. Although I want to act calm and collected, I'm unable to hide how shocked I feel staring at his uniform. "You're a fireman?"

He pulls down his shades and smiles charmingly. "I am. Proud member of the Crested Butte Fire Protection Division for six years now."

I swear the moment I gaze into Lance's eyes, I forget—for just an instant—I'm dangling thirty feet in the air.

What's in a Name?

Lance

As we pass through the first tower, Avery looks like she is about to hyperventilate when the carrier is jostled as it passes through the first tower.

"Everything okay?"

She nods stiffly.

Clearly, it's not, but I don't force the issue. "In case you were curious, Moonbeam is a ferocious eater."

Her eyes soften when she asks, "Moonbeam? Is that what you named her? I've been wondering how the kitten was doing."

I frown. "Didn't you get my note? I left it at your door last night after my shift ended."

Avery shakes her head. "I guess the wind must have taken it. The gusting wind was fierce last night." She then looks at me hopefully. "So, she's doing well?"

"She is," I assure her. "She's vaccinated and has a clean bill of health."

"I'm glad to hear that. So, did you find someone to take her?"

"Not yet, but I'm hopeful."

She smiles with relief. "I love the name, by the way. It's perfect for her."

"I thought so, too." Remembering the halo around the moon last night, I share, "The moon actually inspired the name. Did you see it last night?"

"I did!" Her eyes suddenly light up. "The full moon was magical with that halo around it."

Damn…I love the way her eyes sparkle.

In the silence that follows, I notice her tensing up again. Wanting to keep the conversation light, I ask, "So, what did you end up doing last night?"

"I read a book…" Avery bites her lip, and I suddenly notice tears welling up in her eyes. "To tell you the truth…I can't concentrate right now. I…"

She closes her eyes. In a trembling voice, she admits, "I'm deathly afraid of heights."

I look at her in disbelief. "Then what the heck are you doing on this chairlift?"

Avery takes several ragged breaths, her eyes still tightly closed as she struggles to answer me. "I've always been afraid of heights, and…" She opens her pale blue eyes, looking achingly vulnerable when she tells me, "I wanted to conquer it today."

Her bottom lip trembles in the silence that follows.

I feel especially protective of her suddenly. "Avery, what an incredibly brave thing to do."

She looks at me doubtfully.

"I mean it. Facing your fear is the most courageous

things a person can undertake."

I see the look of determination in her eyes as she reaches into her pocket and pulls out a small vial. Opening it with one hand, she dabs a small amount on her wrists and explains, "It's a blend of essential oils I made."

I chuckle. "I've been wondering what that smell was."

"It helps with my inner peace," she says confidently.

"Mind making me some?"

She gives me the slightest of smiles. "I'll see what I can do."

Avery then turns and stares straight ahead. "If I am serious about doing this, I have to be fully present."

I sit beside her in silent support as the chair ascends the side of the mountain. But I notice the white-knuckled death grip she has on the safety bar and the fact that her whole body is visibly shaking.

I long to wrap my arm around Avery to comfort her but refrain, afraid it might make her uneasy. Instead, I try to bolster her courage by saying, "What you're doing today is inspiring."

Halfway up the mountain, the carrier suddenly shudders to a halt and the chair swings back and forth.

"What just happened?" she cries.

"It's nothing," I assure her. "I'm sure someone just needed extra time getting off the lift. It'll start up again in a few."

Her voice breaks when she whimpers, "I'm scared."

The intensity of the fear I hear in her voice calls to me on a soul level. "You're safe with me, Avery," I assure her.

She looks up at me with tears rolling down her cheeks. "Help…"

Wrapping my arms around her is so instinctual that I don't even question it. "I promise I won't let anything hurt you."

She suddenly breaks down in sobs, letting go of the bar and clinging to me.

I hold onto her tight. Her palpable fear mirrors the same terror I often suffer from at night. "It's going to be okay…" I murmur, surprised that the chairlift hasn't started up again.

Keeping one arm around her, I pull my portable radio from my chest harness and call in, asking what the holdup is.

"We're working on a mechanical issue."

When I ask for a time estimate, I notice the maintenance team is evasive with their answer. "We'll have it fixed as soon as possible."

Avery looks up with tears-stained eyes, asking in concern, "What about your emergency?"

I chuckle, recalling the humorous nature of the emergency, and assure Avery, "It isn't life-threatening."

"But what if it becomes life-threatening because you can't reach them in time?"

Touched by her sincere concern, I keep my explanation vague to protect the privacy of the individual. "Although the person may be uncomfortable for a bit, I promise they'll be just fine."

What she doesn't know is that a teenage boy dropped his phone while using the outhouse. In a panic to retrieve it, he squeezed into the hole to try to fish it out and lost his balance. I can't say I am looking forward to servicing the call, but it will make for a good laugh in years to come.

When they call me back on the radio and Avery hears maintenance is waiting for a technician and it will be a half-hour, I watch all of the blood drain from her face.

"Keep me updated," I tell them, looking at Avery with concern.

The terror in her eyes is real when she cries, "I can't do this!"

Wrapping my arms around her tightly, I remove my sunglasses and tell her, "Avery, look at me."

She looks up at me, gasping for breath with tears streaming down her face. I know if I fail to calm her down quickly, she will start hyperventilating. "Take in a deep breath and let it out slowly."

She shakes her head, whimpering, "I feel like I'm going to pass out."

"Avery," I say firmly. "You need to take a deep breath in through your nose and let it out slowly through your mouth. Like this…"

I suck in the cool mountain air and slowly let it out through my mouth. Keeping my gaze fixed on her, I continue breathing slowly in and out and watch with satisfaction as her breath slowly begins to match mine.

"That's it," I encourage her.

But a few seconds later, a bird flies by. She instinctually follows it with her gaze and tenses as it dives toward the ground far below.

"Eyes on me," I command. "Don't take them off of me."

She nods.

I continue the breathing exercise until she is able to reconnect with me.

"I'm…so…scared," she whispers.

"When you face the thing you are most afraid of, you discover the strength to stare it down."

She looks at me in wonder. "That's profound."

I smirk self-consciously. "I wish I could take credit for it, but I was paraphrasing Eleanor Roosevelt."

Her light chuckle warms my heart.

"When you are ready, Avery, look up at the mountain peak." Speaking from experience, I tell her, "It's important not to look down but to stay focused on the direction you are headed."

She sniffs as she wipes her eyes. "That almost sounds like spiritual advice."

"Take it however you want it," I chuckle. "The fact is, you came on this chairlift for an important reason, and I would hate for you to miss out on the beauty of this mountain—or the strength of your courage."

"Thank you…" she murmurs, taking a deep breath before looking up at the peak.

When I lean forward to gently wipe a stray tear from her cheek, I suddenly feel her lips against mine as she kisses me. The surge of passion that passes between us is exhilarating—and electric. Avery melts into my embrace as I kiss her more deeply, and we quickly lose ourselves in the tenderness of the kiss.

When we part, she looks at me with those luminous

eyes, and we each smile at one other.

"Wow…" she murmurs.

When I kiss her again, Avery moans softly as I explore her mouth with my tongue. We kiss for several minutes, our connection becoming more intimate and intense. When we break away again, she whispers in my ear, "Last night I made a wish—"

The radio suddenly crackles to life and we hear, "Hey, Macallan! I've got good news for you. Maintenance just finished the repair. The lift will be back up in less than two minutes."

Avery's excited smile transforms into a look of dread. "Wait…your last name is Macallan?"

"Yes…" I answer with amusement, surprised by her reaction.

She suddenly frowns and looks back up at the mountain.

"Why so you ask?"

"Do you have any brothers, Lance?" she asks in a strained voice.

I chuckle when I answer. "I do. I have four of them, actually—"

The lift springs back to life, and Avery lets out a terrified shriek.

When I reach out to steady her, she tenses in my arms. I let go, confused by her odd reaction.

Shutting her eyes tight, she grips the safety bar so fiercely that her knuckles turn white again.

For some reason, it feels as if there is an invisible barrier between us.

I don't understand the sudden change in her mood,

and it leaves me baffled as we continue up the mountain in dead silence.

As we near the terminal, I tell her, "We're almost to the top."

"I'm going to stay on," she mutters through clenched teeth.

"Why?" I ask in concern. It makes no sense, considering her extreme fear of heights.

Keeping her eyes tightly closed, she whispers, "I just want to go home…"

I'm completely caught off guard. "Are you certain you'll be fine going back down alone?"

"Yes."

I'm disheartened by her decision but still respect it. "Okay, but I need you to let go of the bar so I can get off."

Her eyes pop open and she forces her tightly clenched fingers to let go.

The moment the carrier reaches the terminal, I lift the bar and step off, lowering it again for her. Slapping the back of the metal carrier as it pulls away, I call out to Avery, "Take care of yourself."

As it turns around to head back down the mountain, she twists in the seat and meets my gaze. "Goodbye, Lance."

Those words hit me harder than they should, but I smile and wave at Avery.

I hear her frightened squeak when the ground falls away and she begins the journey back down the steep mountain—alone.

As I watch her disappear from view, one of the attendants comes bounding up.

"Hey, Charlie, do me a favor and have someone ready to help the woman I was riding with when she reaches the bottom terminal."

"Sure thing, Lance," he replies, smacking me on the back. "It's a good thing you got up here when you did. That kid has been cussing up a storm inside the latrine."

I groan, dreading the shitshow I'm about to face.

Accidental Kiss

Avery

I can't stop thinking about the kiss…

The moment Lance wiped my tears away with his finger and I saw those lips so close to mine, I couldn't resist. I was drawn to them like a moth to a flame.

Although I've read about epic kisses in romance books, I was completely unprepared for the "fireworks" I felt when our lips touched. Even though it started out tender, the passion simmering between us left me breathless. I remained his willing captive as our kiss intensified and became more intimate and impassioned.

This is my answer, I thought right after the kiss ended. Last night I'd asked for a sign, and it came in the form of this kiss—I felt so certain when it happened.

But his surname is Macallan…and he's a fireman.

The chair bounces, and I am immediately forced back to reality.

I concentrate on my breathing and pop another piece

of gum in my mouth, repeating my new mantra: *I am conquering my fear of heights.*

I feel empowered when I say it.

Although my heart continues to race, and I am desperate for this ride to end, I force myself to be present in the moment.

As we descend, I stare straight ahead and make a conscious effort to genuinely appreciate the majestic peaks around me and the bird's eye view of the small town, while I listen to the wind blowing through the pine trees on the mountain.

Tears roll down my cheeks—tears born of fear and amazement. In all of my life, I have never seen anything so terrifyingly beautiful.

When I finally reach the bottom of the mountain, I'm surprised to see an attendant waiting at the terminal. She smiles pleasantly as she pulls the bar up and helps me out of the chair. Guiding me safely away from the moving chairlift, she points to a bench nearby.

I'm profoundly grateful for the help because my legs feel numb and weak like limp noodles. I walk slowly to the bench and stare at the ground self-consciously as I wipe away the tears on my face. While I try to compose myself, people walk past me to wait in line for the Red Lady.

To my extreme mortification, three different people stop to ask if I'm okay while I sit there. I assure each of them that I am, but one refuses to leave until I accept her extra bottle of water.

After she leaves, I gulp it down. And it's then that it strikes me that this wouldn't happen where I'm from. Being invisible is a natural part of living in a city. Sure, there are always a few individuals willing to stop to offer their help if they see someone in need, but that's the exception to the rule.

Although I find the unwanted attention embarrassing, it does make me feel cared for in this community of strangers, and I am grateful for it. Holding on to that affirming thought, I finish my water and toss the bottle into the recycling bin before making my way back to Ladybug.

I let out a huge sigh of relief the moment I slip into the safety of my car and shut the door. As I stare at the chairlift in front of me, I really can't believe I did it. It wasn't pretty, and I have a jumble of emotions to unpack after what happened with Lance, but I have officially conquered the Red Lady.

As messy as it was, no one can take that away from me.

Feeling raw and completely spent, I buckle up and I turn on my car, anxious to make the short drive to the cabin so I can dive into my soft bed.

As I pull up to a stop sign on an empty side street, Ladybug suddenly stutters and the engine shuts down. I try to start her back up several times, but the car remains silent. She has *never* let me down in all of the years I've owned her. Not wanting to believe something is wrong, I keep trying to restart the car while verbally begging her to start.

Not in an emotional state to deal well with this unexpected complication, I start pounding the steering wheel in a fit of frustration while spewing out a few choice words.

I jump when I hear someone tapping on my window and turn to see an elderly man grinning while his small pug sits on a leash, panting with a joyful grin.

Rolling down my window, I give the man a weary smile. "I apologize for any inappropriate words you may have just heard."

He chuckles. "It looks to me like you're having car trouble. Would you like me to call Gavin?"

I frown. "Who's Gavin?"

"He owns the garage in town. The man can fix anything."

I sigh, realizing I can't go anywhere without help. "Sure. That would be great."

The man gets out his cell phone, smiling at me as he waits for the man to pick up. "Hey, Gavin, there's a young lady who could use your help with her car. She's on Maroon Avenue."

I snort, thinking how ironic it is that my car left me marooned on Maroon Avenue.

The older gentleman furrows his brow for a moment, then asks me, "What's your name, miss?"

"Avery Snow. I'm staying at Punny Peaks." I roll my eyes after saying the name. I realize how ridiculous it sounds when you say it out loud.

After repeating the information, the man hangs up and smiles. "Gavin says he knows who you are and he'll be here in a few minutes."

"How could he possibly know me?" I frown. "I've never even heard of the man."

The gentleman laughs. "It's a small town, Miss Snow."

I let out an exhausted sigh, knowing I shouldn't be surprised by that. Grateful for this man's timely help, I muster a smile and thank him.

"Think nothing of it. Would you like me to stick around until Gavin shows up?"

Realizing I'm on the verge of tears at the moment, I swallow down the lump in my throat and tell him, "I'll be fine, but thanks for the kind offer."

He nods and walks off with his pug trotting happily behind him.

I lay my head back against the headrest and groan, already dreading the cost of the repair bill. I had not factored in my car breaking down when I budgeted for this trip.

Less than five minutes later, I see a tow truck pull up behind me. I immediately notice how beat up the old truck is and start questioning the skill of the mechanic. Glancing through my rearview mirror, I watch a tall man with broad shoulders and a big bushy beard get out of the vehicle. I suddenly wonder if I should have taken the gentleman's offer to wait with me.

I hesitantly get out of my car as the bear of a man walks toward me like he's a linebacker. But then I see his gentle smile when he asks, "Miss Snow, I presume?" and all of my concerns wash away.

Holding out my hand to him, I say gratefully, "Yes.

You must be Gavin, fixer of all things."

His low chuckle is irresistible. I look up as I shake his huge hand, and I'm shocked to see the same crystal blue eyes as the cook at the diner. "No way…"

"No way?" he asks, laughing.

"Are you related to Bram?"

His smile grows wider. "He's my oldest brother."

Another Macallan? You've got to be kidding me.

He must have read something in my expression because he asks in concern, "Did Bram do something to upset you?"

"No, no!" I sputter. "He's an incredible cook."

Gavin strokes his beard, nodding proudly. "He learned from the best."

I'm tempted to ask more about Annie but decide it's best if I don't dive any deeper into the Macallan Family, so I quickly change the subject. "I sure hope you can help me with my little bug. She's never given me any trouble until today."

"Happy to." He approaches my metallic blue VW with a look of appreciation. "I see you have a 2005. That year has a great track record."

I smile as I look at my car. "I've loved her ever since the day I bought her."

After I explain what happened when the car died, he pops the hood to check the engine. Wiping his hands on the red towel in his pocket, he asks for the keys. After I hand them over, I watch in amazement as this goliath of a man squeezes into my small vehicle. After trying to start it several times, he taps the horn twice and smiles as he maneuvers himself back out.

"You have a happy car there."

I chuckle. "She and I have shared many good times together."

Staring thoughtfully at my VW, he tells me, "I suspect you have a bad CPS."

A van pulls up behind us and Gavin waves for them to go around. The family inside waves excitedly back at him as they pass.

He chuckles at me, looking embarrassed by their attention. I can't help wondering what it is about this gentle giant that caused them to react that way.

"I'd like to tow your car to my garage after I drop you off at Punny Peaks."

"Oh, no! You don't need to go to all that trouble. I'll just call an Uber."

"Uber's not really a thing here," he chuckles. "Besides, it'll be no trouble. I'd be honored to help our new librarian."

I feel the need to correct him. "I'm actually still deciding if I'm going to take the job."

Gavin nods, saying nothing as he proceeds to hook up my car to the tow truck. After he hitches the Beetle, I follow him to the tow truck and climb into the cab.

On our short drive to the motel, Gavin looks at me kindly. "I hope you stay."

I smile, touched by his simple request. Turning to stare out the window, I think how it's interesting that each brother I've met is vastly different. Despite that, based on what I heard in the library, there is one thing they all share.

Needing to know if it's true, I look back at Gavin.

"So, just out of curiosity, are any of your brothers married?"

He snorts as if he finds the question funny. "No, ma'am."

I nod, letting that sink in.

Lance is one of the Macallan brothers.

He is also a firefighter.

While that might be sexy to some, his profession invites heartbreak. Every time one of them goes on an emergency call, they have no idea what they will face.

Some never make it home.

That risk frightens me.

I nod to myself, accepting the truth. I cannot have feelings for Lance Macallan.

Unable to resist the intense chemistry we share, I'll just have to stay far away from the man.

Close Call

Lance

Immediately after returning to the firehouse, I ask my pal Montoya to cover for me while I head to the shower and strip off my clothes. Throwing them in the washer, I lay out a new set of station wear. I need to be prepared in case the tone drops, announcing an emergency call, while I'm taking a shower.

I can't scrub away the stench from my skin fast enough! Despite the horrifying smell, I have to say that pulling the teenager out of the bottom of the outhouse has to be one of the funniest and most disgusting things I've done in my career.

While I'm scrubbing down, I hear Moonbeam sitting outside the door, meowing plaintively like a child crying for its mama. The crew at the firehouse have been understanding about me bringing her here for my shift and assured me they won't breathe a word to Fire Chief Higgins.

But, naturally, they give me plenty of shit about it.

The fact that I've shaved off my beard and now have a kitten has them convinced I'm going soft. I don't mind their razzing, because if the shoe was on the other foot, I'd be thinking the same thing.

Racing to finish, I'm grateful when I make it out of the shower without interruption. However, while I'm toweling myself off, I notice Moonbeam has stopped meowing.

Before I have a stitch of clothing on, the tone drops.

"Shit!" I groan. I quickly slip on my briefs and socks, sweep up the rest of my uniform, and rush to the door so I can put them on in the truck.

The moment I step out, I'm confronted by a very angry Chief Higgins holding Moonbeam in his hands.

I plant a grin on my face. "What are you doing here, Chief?"

He holds the squirming kitten out to me and demands, "What is the meaning of this?"

I immediately drop my clothes and grab the kitten from him. "She's a rescue, Chief. The vet said she might die without proper care, so I had no other option."

"I don't care what the vet said!" he roars. "The rule in this station is no animals. There are *no* exceptions."

I notice all of my chums shifting comfortably. I don't think any of us have ever seen Chief Higgins this upset before.

"I will *not* tolerate insubordination," he barks, staring at the kitten.

I put Moonbeam behind my back, telling him, "I understand, Chief. I'll make a call right now and get her out of here."

"You should have done that before, Macallan."

I'm sweating bullets, realizing his tone does not bode well for me, and I can't help but think about Finn's warning last night. I can't afford to have a blemish on my record if I ever want to make lieutenant.

"I'm questioning your future here."

Fire Chief Higgins turns to the rest of the crew. "Every person here deserves a warning for willfully covering this up."

Silence fills the station.

I feel sick knowing that I've put my entire team at risk of disciplinary action.

Still in my underwear, I set the kitten down to face the Chief. "This is one hundred percent on me. I didn't give them a choice."

"You're wrong, Macallan. Everyone had the choice to pick up the phone and call me." He frowns, adding with a growl, "But they didn't."

Chief Higgins then laughs sarcastically, "The irony of all of this is that I came to personally commend you all for winning the Safety Performance Award for our district."

He turns and addresses all of us. "Our team is built on trust. It's the glue that has kept us safe all these years. It is the *only* thing that matters. Why would you allow a mere feline to compromise my trust in you?"

We all answer in unison, "Sorry, Chief."

"Well, 'sorry' isn't going to cut it," he snarls.

Knowing that none of this would be happening if I hadn't brought the kitten into the firehouse, I plead, "Respectfully Chief, I'm the problem here. I should bear the weight of their punishment as well as my own."

He narrows his eyes, nodding slowly as if contemplating my suggestion. I have a sickening feeling that I may lose my job today.

Montoya speaks up, "Chief Higgins, you're right. Trust is essential for our team. It's the reason I come to work each day confident that I'll return home. Macallan is someone we all trust with our lives. Our team would be compromised without him, even for one day."

Everyone grunts their approval.

Chief Higgins considers Montoya's words for a moment, then steps closer to me, getting up in my face. "Since Montoya is convinced that you are an integral part of the team, I will let you both prove it to me. You'll be in charge of the latrines for the remainder of the year. I want them to be as spotless as your integrity from this day forward."

I look him in the eye, grateful he's giving me this chance, as well as for Montoya's brave intervention on my behalf. "I will not disappoint you, Chief."

"I will not look the other way next time," he growls.

"Understood, sir."

Glancing down at the kitten rubbing against my leg, he snarls, "Get rid of the cat, *now*! You have ten minutes."

I snatch up Moonbeam while Chief Higgins turns to address the crew, telling them, "Rather than a celebration to mark winning the award as I had planned, I've decided you'll all scrub down this station from top to bottom."

Still in my underwear, I watch everyone race to get the cleaning supplies. Embarrassed by the trouble I've caused, I grab my phone and call Malcolm, the one brother we all go to whenever we're in a jam.

Thankfully, he's quick to answer. "Hello?"

"Hey, Malc, it's an emergency."

"Is someone hurt?" he immediately asks with concern.

I lower my voice. "No. But I almost got myself fired just now."

"Tell me what happened."

Already, I feel better knowing Malcolm's on the case. "Look, I don't have time to explain. I need to get a kitten I brought to the station out of here right now or Chief Higgins is going to fire me."

"You're kidding, right?"

I look over at my Chief scowling at me and whisper, "I'm deadly serious, brother. I need you here in five minutes. That'll give me enough time to get clothes on."

"*What?* Never mind, I don't want to know…"

"Can you come?" I plead.

"I'm sorry, Lance. My client just walked through the door."

"You're the only one close by! I'd ask Gran, but she's deathly allergic to cats."

"I wish I could help you, but I can't right now. You'll find someone else. You've got this."

After he hangs up, I look at Chief Higgins and fake a grin. "I'm on it, Chief!"

Throwing my uniform on with the lightning-fast speed only firefighters possess, I rush outside with Moonbeam and jump into my truck. The only person I can think to ask is Avery. Even though I don't understand what happened on the chairlift, I know she wouldn't turn Moonbeam away.

Racing down the dirt road, I pull into the parking lot, my tires kicking up dust. I know the clock is ticking. Running up to her cabin, I pound on the door. "Avery, Moonbeam needs you!"

The moment Avery opens the door, I feel a rush of relief. "I'm sorry. I don't have any time to explain, but I need you to take Moonbeam."

I thrust out the kitten to her. Avery hesitates for a moment before taking the kitten and cradling her in her arms. Rightfully confused, she asks, "What's going on, Lance?"

"I wish I had time to explain…" I glance at my watch anxiously. "But, I'm about to get fired if I don't make it back to the firehouse right now."

I leave her standing there with her mouth wide open as I run back to my truck. I lower the window as I pull out and shout, "I'll explain later!"

I glance at the time again and hit the gas, spraying gravel everywhere.

I feel a strange peace settle over me as I head back to the fire station. Even though it was ridiculously brief, seeing Avery was exactly what I needed.

While Montoya and I scrub down the toilets and show-ers in utter silence—per Chief Higgins's strict orders—I am free to think about Avery.

It was clear when she decided to stay on the chairlift instead of getting off with me that something was seriously wrong. But for the life of me, I can't under-stand what it might be when the two of us hit it off so well.

When I think about our kiss, everything feels right. The chemistry was intense, and so was the connection I felt with her. The fact that Avery initiated the kiss proves that the feelings I have for her are reciprocated.

I close my eyes, wanting to breathe in her scent and taste those lips again. I'm hungry to discover the secret places that will tease and please Avery to distraction.

My cock gets hard just thinking about it, and I have to shake my head to clear my thoughts. Needing the distraction, I turn my attention back to the toilet bowl I am scrubbing. It's imperative that I *not* think about Avery or the kiss. Otherwise, the obvious response my thoughts are having are guaranteed to humiliate me in front of Montoya.

Instead, I reflect on the chairlift ride with Avery, try-ing to figure out where things went wrong between us. Thinking back on our conversation, I dissect every detail of the ride up the mountain, trying to pinpoint what I might have said to upset her.

Everything comes back to one moment...

After the radio call came in and she asked if my last name was Macallan, her entire demeanor changed—but it doesn't make any sense to me. Our family is well respected in this town. We may come off as an odd bunch to outsiders, but my dad is a pillar of the community, and he raised his sons to follow in his footsteps.

Then it hits me—Killian.

That man has had it out for my father for years. And with Maisey destroying his fucking pumpkin, he's been itching to start a fight. Is it possible he got to Avery somehow?

No…I don't believe it. I can't see Avery being that gullible when the man is obviously unhinged.

The only other thing I recall is the shocked look on her face when she realized I was a firefighter. It's something women either love or hate.

It's a dangerous profession.

While I kneel beside the damn toilet I'm scrubbing, visions of my nightmare suddenly flash in my mind and I vividly re-live that terrifying moment just before I wake up from the dream. With sweat beading on my skin and my hands now shaking, it takes everything in me not to scream even though I can feel the fire scorching my skin.

I've always known I'm living on borrowed time. Maybe Avery can sense that about me.

Constantly facing the possibility of death is a both a blessing and a curse. The moment a person truly understands that their time on this Earth is numbered, every day becomes an adventure that is meant to be savored.

It's the reason I don't hold back on *anything*. I live life with passion, wanting to explore everything the world has to offer. That's how I've always lived my life.

But the connection I experienced with Avery? *That* is dangerous—not for me, but for her.

My career is not a choice, it's my destiny.

The Claw of Attraction

Avery

A couple of hours after Gavin drops me off and tows Ladybug to his garage, I'm startled to hear Lance pounding on the cabin door and shouting about Moonbeam.

I rush to the door when I hear the urgency in his voice. Opening it, I find him standing there looking devastatingly handsome.

Thrusting Moonbeam toward me, he states I need to take her. Bewildered, I grab the sweet little puffball from him and press her against my chest.

I can't imagine what has Lance so agitated and ask, "What's going on?"

He mutters something about possibly being fired as he runs back to his red truck. He hightails it out of the parking lot, spewing gravel and yelling out of his window, "I'll explain later!"

Stunned, I stand in the doorway watching the dust

settle and wonder what the heck just happened.

I shut the door in a daze and place Moonbeam on the bed, then sit down beside her. Petting her soft fur, I mutter, "I sure wish you could talk and tell me what just happened."

Despite my resolve not to get involved with Lance, seeing him again has made one thing clear—I've already fallen for the guy.

Between his swoon-worthy kiss, his dramatic rescue of Moonbeam, and the thoughtful way he helped me avert my panic attack on the chairlift, I can't help having feelings for the man.

I jump when I hear another knock on the door. Wondering if Lance has returned, I run to open it.

"Guid afternoon, Miss Snow."

I can't hide the surprise on my face when I see Clara standing on the porch holding a large basket. Knowing that pets aren't allowed in the cabin, I squeeze through the door and shut it behind me.

"What have you got in the basket?"

Clara grins as she hands it to me. "A certain Macallan mentioned you might be needing some supplies."

Wondering what she means, I open the basket and let out a relieved laugh. "So, you know about the kitten."

She nods. "Aye, Lance just called me."

"I'm glad, because I know your motel has a strict no-pets policy."

"And for guid reason, lass. I'm severely allergic to cats."

I crinkle my eyebrows. "Then why did you allow it?"

Clara's eyes soften when she tells me. "Lance is a

guid soul. He can be a wee bit rash at times, but his heart is always in the right place…" She chuckles. "He also promised to do a detailed cleaning of the cabin after you leave, and he mentioned somethin' about having to do the same at the fire station."

I frown. "Do you think he got in trouble because of the kitten?"

She tilts her head. "I know Chief Higgins is not a fan of animals."

I suddenly feel guilty, realizing Lance put himself in jeopardy at work because of the kitten.

"Are you worried about him, lass?" she asks with a knowing smirk.

I roll my eyes, pretending otherwise.

But she is too astute. "Aye, I know that look…" Glancing at my left hand, she asks boldly, "Are you looking to marry?"

"No!" I blanch, surprised she would be so forward in asking such a question.

"You cannae do better than marrying one of my grandsons," she insists. "They come from good stock and are loyal to those they love."

Deciding to be equally direct, I ask her, "And are any of them married?"

Clara clicks her tongue. "Nae a one. It's quite the topic of discussion in the town."

Knowing I'm guilty of listening to that gossip, I set what I've heard aside and pretend I know nothing about it. Wanting to hear about the Macallans from someone who knows them best I tell her, "I'm certainly surprised Bram remains single being such a wizard in the kitchen."

The pride she feels is easy to see in her eyes. "That boy learned everything he knows about cooking from Annie. It's hard to believe it's been over twenty years since she's passed…"

I suddenly realize that whoever Annie is, she can't be Bram's lost love like I first assumed. "Who is Annie, Clara?"

Instead of answering, Clara takes my hand and pats it gently as she leads me to a picnic table down near the river. She looks out at the fast-moving water for several moments before she takes a seat beside me. "I don't normally share this with others, but I like you, Miss Snow."

I smile warmly at her. "I feel the same, Clara.

"After the boys' sweet mam passed away, they became a tight-knit bunch. Those five have been taking care of each other ever since."

My heart suddenly aches for the brothers—especially Lance.

Clara's eyes shine fiercely when she tells me, "I left my beloved Scotland to be with my grandchildren. Although my son Leith has done an excellent job raising his boys, *no one* should have to parent alone."

I'm moved by the sacrifice she made for her grandsons and tell her, "Although I've only met three of them so far, they seem like exceptional men."

"Oh, they are, lass," she agrees proudly.

Clara is silent for a long moment before she continues. "Each boy has been given a gift." She declares with grandmotherly conviction, "And they share them with the people of the town as guid Scotsmen should."

"In what way?" I ask her, intrigued by her assertion.

Her voice overflows with love when she says, "Bram shares his culinary gift every day at the diner. Malcolm is a genius with numbers and uses his gift to invest in the community as their banker. Gavin has always had a way with mechanical things, as you already know." She winks. "Whereas Finn is more ethereal and expresses it through his artistry with stone."

"And Lance?"

She looks at me and smiles. "You've already experienced it, lass."

I nod. I'm certain she means his protective nature, but all I can think about is the passion behind his kiss.

Clara takes my hand and squeezes it warmly. "I hope you'll stay for the Fall Festival, Miss Snow. It is a wonderful way to get to know the community, and it may even give you the clarity you need."

"Flora Elwood mentioned it to me. When is the festival?"

"October 7."

"Well, that's a shame. I leave that morning."

"I know, I made yer reservation," she laughs. "But I wanted to personally invite ye to the festival. It's a big event for the community, and one not to be missed. I'll be there running one of the many other carnival booths. We also have local bands, a hay bale maze, as well as fall-themed competitions."

Still uncertain if I want to commit, I choose not to respond to her invite and instead ask a question. "When you say fall-theme competitions, that wouldn't happen to include a certain orange squash, would it?"

I can't miss the glint in her eye. "Aye, it most certainly does."

Remembering how rude the man was to Clara at the office, I ask, "Did your son's cow really destroy his pumpkin like he claimed?"

"I can't say since I wisnae there," she answers. "But it would serve that bampot right! Maisey was once his cow, but Killian sold her to a slaughterhouse when she stopped producing milk months after he purchased her."

My jaw drops. "That's terrible!"

"When my son Leith heard about it, he bought her from the slaughterhouse the day they came to collect the poor thing. Turns out, Maisey was allergic to something in the cheap cattle feed that fool was giving her. It only took a couple of weeks of eating grass and clover before Maisey started producing again."

Clara raises her chin proudly when she announces, "And wouldn't you know? Maisey is the best-producing dairy cow Leith has ever had."

"I suppose Maisey was simply getting even when she trashed his pumpkin."

She laughs, "That she was, lass."

Clara checks her phone, then looks at me apologetically. "I need to head back to the office and call my Scabby Queen Ladies. We're trying to decide on a potluck theme for our next game night."

"Scabby Queen Ladies?"

She grins when she tells me, "They're a bunch of women I meet up with every Wednesday to play my favorite card game, Scabby Queen. We snack on good food and have a blether as we play. But the best part for me is that whoever loses must play truth or dare." She bursts out laughing. "It makes for great shenanigans!"

"I can only imagine."

I follow Clara as we head back to the lodge. I stop at my cabin while she goes on to the office. I'm grateful for this talk with her. It's given me much-needed insight into Lance and his brothers.

When I open the door, I find Moonbeam curled up on my pillow. She lifts her head and makes the sweetest mew when she sees me. Unable to resist her cuteness, I walk over to the bed and lie down beside her.

Rather than grabbing a book, I decide to pick up my journal instead. Feeling inspired by today's events, I indulge in a little fantasy involving Old Rock and let my imagination run wild.

The library has been humming with activity but, with the day finally winding down, there are only a few patrons left in the building.

I'm upstairs shelving books when the fire alarm sounds. Thankfully, I know the fire station is only two blocks away. Putting all fear aside, I immediately start directing everyone downstairs and out the exit in an orderly fashion.

The fire engine sirens surround the building in minutes, frightening an older woman I am helping down the stairs. In her panic, she pushes me away while I try to steady her. I twist my ankle as I start to fall…

Into the arms of a fireman.

"I got you."

I look up to see the most beautiful seafoam eyes.

Flora runs over excitedly, telling me that it's only a false alarm.

When Lance sets me down, I wince in pain. Immediately sweeping me back into his arms, he asks Flora where I can lie down.

She guides him to a private room with a table and sofa. Laying me down gently on the couch, he takes off my shoe to assess my injury, running his hands lightly over my ankle.

My body responds to his touch far too readily and I bite my lip.

Lance looks up with a crooked grin. "I think you might need ice."

I nod my agreement.

He disappears from the room, returning a short time later with a small bag of ice.

I watch as he kneels to administer the ice pack. I can't help but let out a gasp when the cold ice touches my skin.

"Better?" he asks in a husky voice.

I smile, answering breathlessly. "Yes."

"Does anything else hurt?"

I nod, pointing to my lips.

Lance gives me a sexy smirk and gets up to discreetly shut the door before returning to the couch. Taking off his protective gear, he kneels beside me and murmurs. "Let me see if I can help with that…"

The simple act of his lips pressing against mine makes me crazy, and I moan softly into his mouth.

Lance tilts my head back, leaving a trail of fiery kisses down my throat. In an official fireman tone, he tells me, "I need to listen to your heart."

"Please," I agree, panting with anticipation.

Lance slowly unbuttons my blouse and slips it from my shoulders. He lays his head against my chest, a smile playing on his lips. "You have a rapid heartbeat."

"I do…"

"Shall we make it beat even faster?"

I nod enthusiastically.

Pushing back the material of my bra, he lowers his head and lightly kisses my nipple before encasing it with his mouth.

Goosebumps rise on my skin as he begins to suck on it.

The man drives me wild, and all I want is to feel him moving inside me, rocking my body with his deep, powerful thrusts—

Moonbeam bumps against my journal, interrupting my prose as she innocently rubs her cheeks against the edge of the book.

If she only knew what I was writing.

My imagination is so vivid that I can still feel his kisses trailing across my skin.

With my heart racing, I close my journal and set it back on my nightstand before petting the impish cat.

First Date?

Lance

As soon as my forty-eight-hour shift ends, I head back to the motel to retrieve the kitten. I'm unsure what kind of reception I'll get, considering I threw Moonbeam in Avery's face and drove off.

She has every right to be angry with me.

But when I knock on the door, she answers, looking as if she's pleased to see me.

"You wouldn't happen to be illegally harboring a kitten, would you?" I ask.

Her light laughter sets me at ease. Something seems to have changed, and I feel the natural connection flow between us like before.

"Your grandmother told me you almost lost your job because of Moonbeam."

I shrug. "Couldn't be helped. I knew the rules at the stationhouse, but I hadn't found anyone to take her yet."

"I'm sorry you were put in that position, Lance."

"Not your fault. But I certainly appreciated your help." I hold up the purple flower I've been hiding behind my back.

She smiles as she takes it from me. "You didn't need to do that. I was happy to help."

"Well, I did kind of spring her on you at the last moment."

Avery opens the door wider, inviting me in. "I know Moonbeam will be happy to see you."

The moment I walk into the cabin, the little fluffball springs off the bed and runs up to me. With a laugh, I scoop her up and listen to her purr. "Here you are, acting all innocent and cute when you almost got me fired today."

"So, what happened when you got back to the fire station?" Avery asks, as she sets the flower in a glass of water and puts it on the two-seater table in the corner.

"Chief Higgins gave me a well-deserved lecture. As a leader on my team, I can't afford to make foolish mistakes that compromise the trust we have in each other."

Avery nods and the two of us stare at the kitten in my arms, enjoying a comfortable silence for several moments.

"About the other day…" Meeting my gaze, I see a blush rise to Avery's cheeks. "I haven't been able to get our kiss out of my mind."

I smile when I hear her confession. "Me either."

She glances down, sweeping her toes on the wood floor nervously. "I still haven't decided if I'm taking the job or not, but I'd like to spend more time with you before I head back to Wichita."

"As in…a date?"

"No," she answers. "I would like to hang out together—casually."

My smile widens. A causal encounter meets both our needs. We can explore the natural connection we share without fear of emotional attachment. "Would you like to visit my brother's studio? Finn's been begging me to check out the sculpture he's been working on for months."

"Do you think he'll mind if I tag along?"

"Nah," I assure her.

Avery's eyes sparkle and a smile spreads across her face. "In that case, I would love to join you."

"I have to take a day off following my 48-hour shift at the firehouse to catch up on sleep, but I'll be back working the desk here on Wednesday. Would you like to meet after my shift ends at eight?"

"Sounds good," she agrees.

"If it's okay with you, I normally stop by the diner to grab a bite to eat when I'm done for the day."

She grins. "Even better. I've been meaning to visit the diner again but have avoided it after putting my foot in my mouth the last time."

I laugh. "How so?"

She looks embarrassed when she tells me, "I loved the food so much that I asked your brother to bring Annie out so I could thank her…" She pauses for a moment. "I had no idea until your grandmother told me that she was your mother and you lost her."

I feel a stab of pain at the mention of my mother's

death.

Avery cries out, "Oh, no! I've done it again. That's the same look your brother gave me. I'm so sorry, Lance."

I pull her to me and smile. "You've done nothing wrong. When you brought up her name, you simply reminded Bram of what he's lost. My brother would never hold that against you—any more than I would."

She looks up at me shyly and nods.

I can see the concern in her eyes and don't want her to dwell on it. "So, I assume you're good with us stopping at the diner so I can grab a quick bite before we head out? You're certainly welcome to order something too as my treat."

She laughs. "This is starting to sound too much like a date." Glancing at the refrigerator, she insists, "I'll just eat a salad before we leave."

A huge yawn unexpectedly escapes my lips, which only reminds me of how tired I am.

"Please, don't let me keep you," Avery insists.

"Yeah, I suppose I'd better head out."

Avery's strawberry curls momentarily cover her face when she leans over to give Moonbeam a goodbye kiss on the head. "Goodbye, Moonbeam." Then she looks up at me and smiles. "Sweet dreams, Lance."

Sweet dreams, indeed.

I wonder if Avery realizes what she does to me? I'm definitely going to need to take a cold shower before bed…

Excited about the night ahead, I watch the minutes slowly tick by on the ancient hall clock Gran brought from Scotland. The moment the clock strikes eight o'clock, I turn the sign in the motel office window to "CLOSED" and lock up the place.

I watch as Avery walks down from her cabin wearing a stylish purple tunic with dark leggings and purple-framed glasses to match.

She's dressed way fancier than I am.

I chuckle as she approaches. "I thought this wasn't a date," I tell her, glancing down at my jeans and flannel shirt.

"It's not," she answers with a grin.

Not about to complain when Avery's looking so fine, I gesture to my truck. "I figure I'll drive since I know where we're headed."

"I appreciate that since I don't have my car."

I open the door for her, glancing around the parking lot. "Hasn't Gavin fixed it yet?"

"He says it's a simple repair, but he spent time shopping around to get me a really good price on the crank sensor thingy. It's supposed to get here tomorrow."

I smile, knowing the exact part she means, but I prefer her description of it. "Gavin's does have serious connections in the automotive world. It's a boon for all of us living in this small mountain town."

"Well, I'm definitely grateful to him. Because I wasn't prepared for any repair bills on this trip," she says with a laugh.

I pull into the diner parking lot and have to search for an open spot. It is a point of family pride that the restaurant has remained a popular hangout in Crested Butte. Although my mother's recipes are part of its success, it's my oldest brother's dedication to his craft that has kept the place humming all these years.

I notice Avery hesitates for a moment when I open the door. Knowing she's uneasy about seeing Bram again, I escort her to the counter. As we make our way, I spot several shocked expressions from locals who have yet to see me without my beard. I must admit, it's been a source of endless amusement for me.

Since everyone at the diner is familiar with my schedule, there's always an open stool for me. Tonight, I insist that Avery take it, while I stand beside her.

Ruby sees us and slides over two glasses of water, giving me a wink.

The moment Bram walks out of the kitchen, he stops dead in his tracks and grins. "I still can't get used to your face without a beard."

Then he sees Avery and his smile grows even wider. "I was wondering when I would see you again."

"I'm so sorr—" Avery begins.

Holding up his hand to stop her mid-sentence, Bram points to himself. "I am the chef you wanted to thank. So, you can thank me now if you like."

Avery bursts out laughing. The sound of it is so infectious that the other patrons start chuckling as well. I nod to my brother, appreciating the skillful way he handled the potentially awkward situation.

Gushing, Avery tells him, "I was serious about loving your food. Best cinnamon roll I will ever have."

Bram nods. "So, what would you like to order tonight?"

Avery gives him a sheepish look. "I already scarfed down a salad. I just came to keep your brother company while he eats."

I know my brother is not going to let that pass, even though he says nothing to her. Bram then turns to me, "What'll you have tonight, little stinker?"

I roll my eyes, hearing his nickname for me. As the oldest brother, whenever my father had to work in the field, Bram got stuck potty training me after my mother passed. Naturally, he has never let me forget it.

"I'm hungry for a plate of Maw's Chicken-Fried Steak."

"Gotcha."

After he heads back into the kitchen, Avery turns in her stool to face me. "Thank you."

"For what?"

"For bringing me here. I was worried about coming back, but your brother made me feel welcome."

I point to her forehead. "As a bookworm, you have a tendency to get too inside your head."

She smirks. "What makes you think that?"

"My brother Malcolm is that way, too."

Avery keeps her gaze on me as she drinks her water, leaving me to wonder what she's thinking. That's the intriguing part of spending time with someone new. You don't know the person well enough to pick up on their wee traits yet.

Setting down her glass, she says in amazement, "I swear, even the water tastes better up here."

"And it should when it comes straight from the heavens—no middleman involved."

She chuckles, staring at her glass of water. "I suppose that's true."

Davy, one of the old-timers who owns the hardware store, folds his newspaper and stands up. "Go and take my seat, boy."

"Oh, no. I'm fine standing," I assure him.

"I insist." He waves at Ruby. "Can you box up the rest so I can take it home?"

"Sure thing, hon!"

Davy grins at me. "Take it from a man my age, when you have the opportunity to dine with a pretty lady, you should enjoy it."

I appreciate Davy's kind gesture and nod.

Excusing myself, I tell Avery that I'm headed to the bathroom to wash my hands. As I pass by Ruby, I tell her to put Davy's meal on my tab. I figure kindness should be paid with kindness, especially when I know Davy is giving up eating a warm meal just so I can sit beside my "pseudo date."

I return just in time to see Bram set down the huge plate of chicken-fried steak and potatoes, smothered in country gravy. As I expected, he's also brought Avery a treat.

Her eyes grow wide when he places the tall glass filled with raspberries layered between whisky and honey-flavored cream in front of her.

"What's this?" she cries out happily.

"Cranachan," Bram informs her. "It's a family favorite. On the house."

"Oh, I can't—"

"It's rude to refuse a gift from the cook," he states, heading back to the kitchen.

I laugh once he's out of earshot, telling her, "My brother assumes this is a date…"

Her eyes twinkle merrily. "It kinda feels that way despite our best intentions."

I hold up my water glass to her, curious to see what the evening will bring. "Shall we make a toast?"

With a mischievous smile, Avery picks up her plastic glass and clicks it against mine. "Here's to the night ahead, little stinker."

I smile, enjoying her peal of laughter even though it's at my expense.

At the same time, I think to myself, *Bram is going to pay dearly for that…*

Butterflies

Avery

I'm amazed by how quickly Lance can scarf down the large plate of food. When he notices me watching, he chuckles. "When you work as a fireman, you learn to eat rapidly in case there's an emergency."

"I bet you're the first one finished at your station."

"Oh, no. I can't hold a candle to Montoya," he snorts. "The man is an animal."

I smile as I watch him take another huge bite. It's hard to believe Lance can pack so much in with one forkful. I'm not only impressed by his enthusiasm, but also by the way he groans in appreciation while eating the tasty dish.

A thought flashes in my mind, and I can't help wondering if he's as equally enthusiastic in bed.

"I have to say it's an impressive skill," I tell him, trying hard not to fantasize about Lance looking up from between my legs with those hungry green eyes.

I sigh softly and take another spoonful of my dessert, licking the extra cream off the spoon absentmindedly while my mind willfully wanders. I get so lost in that sensual daydream that I'm startled when I hear the clinking sound of his fork hitting the clean plate.

"Ready to meet the artist in the family?"

I'm quick to jump off the stool. "Absolutely!"

"Eat and run, huh?" Bram teases Lance, picking up his empty plate and wiping the counter.

"You know me, brother." Lance grins, resting his hand on my back as he escorts me out of the diner.

I notice many of the patrons staring at us with obvious interest as we make our way to the door. I can just imagine the tongues that will wag as soon as we're out of earshot.

"You made quite a stir back there," Lance comments as he helps me into his truck.

"What did I do this time?" I laugh.

Lance stops and gazes into my eyes, lightly touching my nose with his fingertip. "You're incredibly sweet, and your freckles are too dang cute."

I'm startled by the way my body responds to the simple contact. I follow him with my eyes as he shuts my door and walks around the red hood of his truck. I feel a bit light-headed, having never been this attracted to a man before.

I find it both thrilling and somewhat intimidating.

Sliding into the driver's seat, Lance starts up the truck and I smile when I feel the seat beneath me vibrate from the powerful engine.

He states as he backs up, "Unlike my other brothers,

Finn is a loner, preferring nature over most people."

I'm now even more intrigued about meeting his brother. Based on what I overheard at the library, I assumed the town's famous artist lived in a posh house. It was the whole reason I dressed up for the evening. "You make him sound like a hermit."

"He is to some extent. But if you're expecting an unkempt person with no social skills who constantly mumbles to himself, then you'll be disappointed." He snorts, adding, "Although, now that I think about it, Finn does mumble a lot..."

I'm excited as we head out of town and drive around the base of the mountain in the moonlight. It still amazes me just how small the town of Crested Butte really is. I'm used to Wichita, a city with almost four hundred thousand people in it.

Glancing up at the night sky through the truck window, I'm stunned by how dark the sky is here without all the bright city lights. It feels like a different world to me.

I experience a thrill of adventure when Lance turns off the main road and starts down a narrow dirt road in the dark, passing over a section of bumpy grating meant to stop cows. "Does your brother own a ranch?" I ask in surprise.

"No," he chuckles. "Finn bought the place from an old-timer and uses the barn for his art studio."

"That's cool..." I look down at my outfit, finally realizing how overdressed I am when we pull up a long gravel road. Ahead, I spot the looming silhouette of a large, weatherworn barn with warm yellow light pouring from the open pocket door. Turning off the truck, Lance looks at me and says with a playful smirk, "Don't make any sudden movements."

I laugh nervously, certain Lance is joking, but secretly thinking, *What if he's not...*

The moment I enter the barn, everything I expected falls away when I see the incredible masterpiece made of white marble. The towering sculpture stands over ten feet high. The moon, expertly sculpted, sits at the top, complete with intricately carved details on its surface. A single moonbeam radiates from the sphere and expands downward. In the middle of the area where the "moonlight" touches the Earth is a carved-out negative space resembling a stately pine tree.

The sculpture is magnificent and emotionally moving. The simple beauty of the piece is amplified by its attention to detail, as well as its sheer size. I stand before it in silent wonder.

Lance stares at it intensely, muttering under his breath, "Interesting choice of subject matter..."

From behind the massive sculpture appears a thin man holding a chisel in his hand. He has a pointed beard and a white forelock in his chestnut hair. He carries an air of mystery and sophistication. I also notice, as he draws nearer, that he has the same blue eyes as Lance's other two brothers.

"You must be Avery," Finn states, switching his chisel to his left hand so he can hold out his right to me.

I grasp it, suddenly feeling awkward as I stand in the presence of someone so talented. At a loss for words, I just squeak, "I am."

His eyes flash with amusement as he shakes my hand

firmly.

Socking his brother in the arm, Lance tells me, "No need to treat Finn like a celebrity. He's a regular Joe like the rest of us."

Finn grins self-consciously. "He speaks the truth."

I shake my head as I glance back at the impressive statue and tell him, "With all due respect, a 'regular joe' could never create something this spectacular." As I stare up at the moon, I add breathlessly, "I certainly know I couldn't…"

Finn walks up beside me. "Actually, it's no different than my brother Bram when he cooks an inspired rendition of Maw's cooking. Or my father, who has an innate understanding of the crops in the fields."

He stares hard at the moon sitting at the top of the statue. "I believe everyone has a calling or 'superpower', as some might call it. My talent just happens to be with stone."

Turning to face me, Finn asks, "What's your calling, Avery?"

I find myself standing mute in the presence of someone so obviously gifted.

Lance steps in and answers for me, "Avery is a librarian." He states it with such admiration and authority that it makes my heart melt.

"Ah…" Finn gives me an appreciative nod. "A worthy calling."

Walking up to the statue to look at it more closely, I tell him, "I've always known I wanted to be a librarian. I can't imagine doing anything else."

He nods. "I believe most children are aware of their

calling early on. But for many people, it becomes clouded by the noise of adulthood."

"Yes!" I agree. "It's one of the reasons I was excited to become a school librarian so I could cultivate their natural love of learning while they're still young."

Lance clears his throat. "Avery has come to Crested Butte to consider taking over Old Rock."

Finn tilts his head. "What attracted you to Old Rock?"

I notice Lance quietly nudge him in the ribs, wanting to spare me from explaining it to his brother.

Although I feel a mixture of sadness and shame saying it out loud, I answer, "I was let go for budget reasons."

Finn furrows his brows. "That's shocking. I can't imagine a school without a fully functioning library."

"It was hard to be let go. However, it led me here and I must say that Old Rock has a unique charm." I admit to Finn, "It makes this decision difficult for me because I have to leave everyone I know behind if I choose to work here."

When I look at Lance, my breath suddenly catches. In those soulful green eyes, I catch a glimpse of something I haven't seen before. A sadness resting just beneath the surface of his carefree exterior. I suspect he hides it with his humor and courageous acts. I feel a connection to that veiled sadness and long to discover the reason behind it.

I notice a flash of movement out of the corner of my eye and turn to see an animal that looks like a miniature fox with incredibly big ears.

"I'm shocked she's come out to meet you," Finn chuckles.

Lance sounds surprised, "She's normally terrified by strangers."

I slowly kneel as I stare at her in wonder. The tiny animal is smaller than a cat, and incredibly adorable with those giant ears. With one forepaw up, she stares at me timidly.

"What's her name?"

"Scotch," Finn answers with pride.

I smile back at her. "I've never seen anything like her before."

"She's a Fennec Fox."

I chuckle, looking back at Finn. "Is that why you got her—because her species is named after you?"

"Not at all," he replies, shaking his head sadly. "I have a friend who is into exotic pets. She couldn't resist those cute ears, but quickly realized these animals are fiercely independent and need plenty of space to explore." Finn looks at Scotch with sympathy. "They are not meant to be house pets."

I can see the affection in his eyes when he tells me, "I couldn't let this innocent creature suffer for my friend's selfish mistake, so I brought her up here so she would have the freedom she deserves."

"It's funny," Lance says, "Because Scotch never leaves Finn's side...except when strangers are around."

The adorable creature takes slow, hesitant steps toward me. When she's close enough, she sniffs me for several moments. She then places her forepaws on my knee so she can sniff my face. I struggle to keep from giggling when her whiskers tickle my skin.

I have to admit, I'm completely enchanted by the sweet animal.

Apparently satisfied with the way I smell, she lowers herself to the ground and runs around in circles several times before trotting over to Lance to give him a hello sniff.

He pats her on the head, and she gives his hand a lick before running over to Finn. I watch the tiny creature launch herself into the air and land in the crook of his arm. Scotch looks up at him lovingly and makes a squeaky purring sound.

"That's the cutest thing I've ever heard!"

Finn smiles at me. "She is cute, isn't she?" As he scratches Scotch on the head, she lowers her ears and continues to purr.

As I'm watching her in rapt adoration, I notice her ears suddenly perk up. She wiggles in Finn's arms excitedly as she stares past me.

It's then I hear the jingling of keys and turn to see Gavin walking up behind me. "I was told you'd be here, Miss Snow, so I decided to bring you your car personally."

"You are far too kind," I gush.

While Gavin hands the keys to me, Scotch flings herself out of Finn's arms and runs up to him, wagging her tail so enthusiastically that her entire body wiggles from head to tail.

The large linebacker of a man gets down on one knee and Scotch jumps up, rubbing her head in his bushy beard. She starts making that adorable purring sound again.

While petting Scotch, Gavin stares at Lance with an odd expression.

"What?" Lance asks, laughing.

"You sure look different without the beard. I hardly recognize you now."

Running his hand over his clean-shaven jaw, Lance says, "Better, I hope."

Gavin shakes his head.

Lance snorts in response and says, "Well, you better get used to it."

Gavin stands up and turns to me. "Would you like to join the three of us for our annual drive up Trappers Way tomorrow?"

I notice Lance shake his head slightly at Gavin. I realize he must be trying to spare me from this awkward situation since his brother assumes we're a couple now. But the truth is, I'd like to hang with Lance tomorrow. "Sure, that sounds like fun—whatever that is."

Lance gives me a worried glance.

Suddenly afraid he *didn't* want me to join them, I sputter, "Unless you'd rather I didn't."

"Of course I'd like you to join us," Lance assures me. "However, I doubt you would enjoy it based on what happened...on the lift."

Understanding suddenly flows through me, and I realize Lance wants to protect me because he knows about my fear of heights. But after conquering the Red Lady, I feel ready for a new challenge and turn to Gavin. "I'd love to go!"

"Excellent. We'll head out at ten so we can take in

the views before the clouds come in later in the afternoon."

I grin, feeling good about this. "I can't wait."

Despite my confidence, I can still see the troubled look in Lance's eyes. But he shrugs, charming me with his smile. "Hey, I'll take any opportunity to spend more time with you."

"I hate to say this, but I'll have to bow out tomorrow," Finn announces, staring at his sculpture. "I'm so close to finishing, and I can't leave until she's complete."

Gavin stares at the massive sculpture and frowns. "It looks done to me."

Finn nods. "She's close, brother. But perfection is the goal."

Shrugging, Gavin heads out, calling to us, "I'll pick up Lance first and then swing by the motel to pick you up."

Finn holds up his chisel, telling the two of us, "If you don't mind, I'd like to get back to work."

Lance snorts. "Kicking us out so soon, brother?"

"What can I say? I'm a slave to my muses."

I try to hide my disappointment as I walk to my VW, sad that my evening with Lance is ending so early. Stuffing down my fears of being rejected, I ask him in a light voice, "Would you like to meet up at my cabin, Lance? We could play cards or something." Then I hold my breath as I wait for his answer.

"I hope you're not the kind of person who gets upset losing. I'm extremely lucky when it comes to cards."

I laugh with relief. "I have no problem watching you lose that lucky streak tonight, Mr. Macallan. I happen to be the Queen of Cards."

"That sounds like a challenge to me, Miss Snow."

"It's not a challenge. It's a promise."

I feel the butterflies start as he turns to get into his truck and I catch his sexy smile out of the corner of my eye.

Jumping into my beloved little car, I smile with satisfaction when I turn her on and hear her familiar purr.

Whatever happens tonight, I am certain of one thing. Even if I don't take the job and never see Lance again, I need to explore this intense attraction I have for him.

I would hate to leave Crested Butte with any regrets, and I know that not taking this chance to know Lance more intimately would be something that would haunt me forever.

Falling Hard

Lance

I follow Avery's VW back to the motel, grateful that it's after hours. To avoid any unnecessary gossip being slung Avery's way, I park my truck behind the motel. The last thing I want is to have her reputation damaged by my obvious attraction to her.

"Keep it cool," I repeat to myself.

The fact is, there is nothing that could keep me away the moment Avery asked me to join her at the cabin. My feelings for Avery are unlike anything I've experienced.

I'm fully aware of the intense chemistry between us, but I know it could easily burn out of control if I let it—and I don't want that. I'm attracted to something far deeper than mere chemicals or appearances. I swear when I look into her eyes I feel as if I've found home.

I shake my head. I'm getting too caught up in my emotions, and grumble to myself, "Get a grip, man."

On one hand, I worry that I'm going to scare her off

by coming on too strong, but there isn't much time before she leaves Crested Butte, and I need her to know how I feel.

However, it goes deeper than that and I know it. Even as a kid, I've felt my days were numbered. The truth is, I have no business loving anyone, much less someone as beautiful as Avery. Still, I cannot resist being drawn to her—it's as if I'm a celestial body being pulled into the sun.

Reminding myself one last time to keep it cool, I walk up to her cabin and knock lightly on the door.

"Come in," Avery calls out.

As I enter, I find her hurrying to tidy up.

"I wasn't expecting company," she laughs as she flits around the small cabin, picking up a few errant dishes. "I'm normally tidier than this…"

I look around the cabin as I take a seat on the small sofa. "The place looks perfectly clean to me."

I glance at the purple flower on the table and ask her, "Do you like flowers, Avery?" I plan to gauge her reaction to determine whether I should send more.

"I love them," she says smiling as she glances at the flower in the water glass. "My favorite are sunflowers. They always fill my heart with hope."

Seeing this as an opportunity to entice her to stay, I tell her, "Then you'll enjoy the Wildflower Festival we have every year in July. The open fields are covered with sunflowers."

Her eyes light up. "I remember reading about the festival on the internet. Is it a big deal?"

"It's been going since 1986. Thousands of people

come from all over the world to visit during the peak of the wildflower season."

"I bet it's beautiful."

I nod casually, secretly hoping she'll stay so I can take her next year.

Avery walks to the nightstand and picks up a deck of cards lying there. "I like to play Clock Solitaire when I'm alone and I just want to veg."

"Can't say I've ever heard of it."

"It's a simple game. You put the cards in twelve piles so they look like a clock and then turn them over, placing each card in its corresponding space on a clock face. It's just a silly game that doesn't take any skill, but I find it relaxing."

Walking up to me, she asks, "What do you like to play?"

I smirk. "Actually, I'm not much of a card player. The sad truth is I take after my granny, who is the reigning champion of losing at Scabby Queen. It's uncanny how unlucky Gran is at the game. She honestly excels at being terrible."

Avery laughs, then scrunches up her nose. "If you don't play cards, why did you come?"

I shrug. "I wanted to spend more time with you."

She smiles as a blush rises to her cheeks. I find it utterly charming. "Rather than playing cards, how about we just talk?"

Avery scoffs. "I'm not that interesting."

I shake my head. "Why don't you let me be the judge of that…?"

We spend the next two hours chatting. Talking to

Avery comes so naturally that I swear it feels like I've known her all of my life. Initially, we keep our discussion light and conversational, but it doesn't take long before I have her laughing hard by telling her about my childhood antics with my brothers. Soon, the poor woman can hardly breathe.

Avery wipes the tears from her eyes, then smiles as she shakes her head. "I adore your humor, Lance. But what I really want is to learn about *you*." She places her hand over my heart. "I want to learn about the man behind that charming smile of yours."

Her light touch short-circuits my brain. I stared into Avery's eyes as I lightly graze her cheek with my fingers. "You're so beautiful…"

She laughs off my compliment. "No, I'm not."

I put my finger to her lips. "Stop. When I give a compliment, I mean it."

Her eyes soften a little. "Thanks."

I lean forward, kissing her lightly on the lips. The moment I feel her melt into my embrace, I kiss her deeper, parting her lips with my tongue.

She pulls back, looking startled.

"Too much?"

Avery gives me a seductive smile. "Not at all. Your kisses are dangerous—but in the best possible way."

"Want to see how dangerous they can get?"

Her eyes flash with excitement. "Although I might combust, I'm definitely game."

Grasping the back of her neck, I explore her mouth with my tongue, reveling in the taste of her. Avery responds with a soft moan that ignites my passion, but I fight my own desire because tonight is all about her.

"Oh, Lance…" she murmurs.

I love that Avery is not timid, returning my fervent kisses with equal ardor.

When I finally disengage from our heated embrace, I stare deep into Avery's eyes. "This may sound forward, but I want to eat your pussy."

Her eyes widen and she bites her lip. "I need you to know that I don't normally do this kind of thing."

"Letting a man pleasure you?" I grin.

Avery laughs as she playfully smacks my shoulder. "I mean that I never rush into intimate relationships."

I nod. "But time is not our friend."

She smiles sadly.

I feel the little hairs rise on the back of my neck. I have the feeling she's already made the decision not to take the job. Even though it will be that much more bittersweet when she leaves, I don't want to miss this opportunity with her.

"Fair warning, Avery. After you feel the magic of my tongue, you may never want to leave."

She smiles as she starts unbuttoning her blouse. "I'll be the judge of that."

She takes it off and I stare at her full breasts bound in a lace bra. I can just make out her areolas peeking through the lacy fabric.

She's so incredibly sexy…

I lean forward to press my lips against her throat as I undo the bra and let it slip to the floor. Avery gasps softly as I slowly leave a trail of kisses down to her breasts. I flick my tongue against her hard nipple, and my cock stiffens in response to her passionate moans.

Turned on by the sound of her desire, I encase her nipple with my lips and suck lightly.

"Oh, God…" she cries out breathlessly.

Moving to her other nipple, I tease it with my tongue. She throws back her head, moaning even louder. Grasping both of her breasts with my hands, I nibble and suck on one nipple while I tease the other with my fingers.

I pull back for a moment, wanting to take in the beauty of her bare chest. Avery's full breasts are sensual, and her nipples are responsive to my touch. "Damn, woman…you're irresistible."

Avery grabs the bottom of my shirt and lifts it up. Eager to get naked with her, I pull the shirt over my head and toss it to the floor. She runs her hands over my chest lustfully. "Damn, you're sexy, Lance," she murmurs, then breathes in deeply and sighs in satisfaction. "You even smell deliciously masculine."

I chuckle and pick her up, carrying her to the four-poster bed. Laying her down on the quilt, I lie down beside her and watch as she excitedly rids herself of her boots and socks.

"Allow me to finish undressing you." As I slip off her leggings, I notice that her lace panties match the lacey bra she was wearing—a good sign that she was hoping for this encounter as much as I was tonight.

Goosebumps rise on Avery's skin when I reach between her legs to find her panties soaking wet. Her soft, rapid breaths only help to fan my desire as I sneak my hand under the waistband of her panties. Swirling my finger over her clit, I kiss her sensuous lips as she moans softly.

I smell her excitement, and long to give her pussy a long, hard lick. But Avery reaches down and rubs her hand over my rigid shaft through my jeans. As turned on by her as I am right now, I can't handle the stimulation and stop her hand.

Shifting my position, I settle down between her legs and smile up at her.

Avery bites her bottom lip, her gaze following my every move as I slowly pull her panties off. I stare at her pussy for the first time, finding the strawberry hue of her mound incredibly hot.

Her clit draws me in, demanding my full attention. I move closer and hesitate for a moment, looking up into Avery's luminous eyes as I take that first long lick. I hear her sharp intake of breath as I taste her.

She tastes of salt and citrus mingled with the scent of her hair. It's an erotic combination. "I could eat you all day, woman."

Avery smiles at me with a ravenous look in her eyes.

When I flick my tongue against her clit, she reacts by raking the skin of my back with her nails, causing chills to course down my spine.

I rub her clit with my fingers, increasing the stimulation, and watch as she throws back her head, thrashing it against her pillow. Encouraged by her passionate moans, I keep up the same pace, mesmerized by the look of ecstasy on her face.

Wanting to feel all of Avery, I caress the outside of her opening with my finger and then slowly penetrate her. Her pussy is hot and wet with desire. It takes everything in me not to give in to my own need.

Keeping our first encounter centered on her tonight, I push my finger deeper into her pussy to find her swollen G-spot and begin sensually caressing it.

Avery moans with more passion, moving her hips in time with my strokes, and encourages me to thrust my finger in and out harder and faster. I pay attention to the rhythm of her body as I seek to please her.

Suddenly tensing, she arches her back and grabs onto the quilt as she pushes her pussy against my hand. There comes a point where I imagine it is not my fingers but my cock claiming Avery, and I groan in satisfaction.

The moment her thighs begin to shake, I know she's getting close to orgasming Wanting to share the moment with her, I move to lay beside her again. Unbuttoning my jeans, I groan when my cock is finally released from its confines.

"Touch me," I groan through gritted teeth.

Avery wraps her hand tightly around my shaft. In response, I close my eyes. "I love that your cock is so hard," she purrs.

We kiss again as I continue to tease her clit and she strokes my shaft. Dangerously close to coming myself, I move down to her nipple and flick it with my tongue with the same rhythm as my fingers play over her clit.

I soon discover Avery's sweet spot based on her passionate moans. Knowing I'm not going to last much longer, I look into her eyes and murmur, "Come with me."

She meets my gaze, responding with a passionate, "Yes!"

Avery closes her eyes and several moments later, her body becomes rigid and she cries out. I feel her pussy contract powerfully around my finger as she thrusts her hips, pressing her mound against my hand.

Watching her climax carries me over the edge. We maintain eye contact as I join her in climax, and we cry out in mutual satisfaction.

"Oh, wow…" she pants afterward. "I've never come at the same time as my partner." She turns to me and grins. "That was amazing!"

"It was," I say with equal enthusiasm.

Avery kisses me on the lips. "I have a confession. Earlier tonight, when we were at the diner, I was imagining this."

"Were you?" I chuckle.

She nods and kisses me again. "Seeing the way you devoured your plate made me curious if you would devour me with that same kind of enthusiasm." She lays her head on the pillow and grins up at the ceiling. "And now I can confirm you certainly can."

I capture her in my embrace and nuzzle her neck. "I'd be happy to anytime."

Avery gazes at me with those pale blue eyes and whispers, "I promise to take you up on that."

With a satisfied smile, I drift off to sleep still holding Avery in my arms…

I stand in front of the old two-story house engulfed in flames. The woman beside me screams hysterically, "My daughter's in there!"

No one in the crowd makes a move to help.

"Somebody please save her!" she cries in desperation.

Her plaintive pleas claw at my soul and I have no choice but to respond.

"Where is she in the house?" I ask, ripping off my T-shirt.

She grabs my arm. "Her room is at the top of the stairs."

As I approach the burning building, I can hear the blaring siren of a fire truck far off in the distance, but I can't afford to wait another second for the crew to arrive.

With adrenalin pumping through my veins, I surge into the house. I have spent my entire life training for this moment.

Covering my nose and mouth with the shirt, I am confronted by black smoke billowing above my head. I can barely make out the stairwell from the foyer. I hunch down to avoid breathing in the smoke as I head to the stairs, knowing every second counts.

Scaling the stairs, I keep my head low to avoid the choking smoke and scorching heat of the fire. Even though I've experienced it before, I am struck by how eerily quiet it is inside the house. The moment I reach the top step, I call out to the girl and immediately hear her high-pitched cries for help.

The smoke is intensely hot on the second level, so I crawl on my hands and knees toward the sound of her voice. As soon as I find the door and enter the bedroom, I close it behind me to give us more time.

Calling out to her again, I follow her muffled cries coming from the other side of the room. Hampered by the thick smoke, I make my way by running my hands over the smooth surface of the wall until I encounter a closet door.

I fling it open. Taking in as deep of a breath as I can, I uncover my mouth and call out to the girl. "Take my hand. Hurry!"

The moment I feel her tiny fingers close round mine, I pull her to me and look into her terrified eyes. "You're safe."

I quickly cover her face with my shirt, then clutch her against me. Crawling back to the bedroom door, I feel it for heat before wrenching it open. The hallway is now completely filled with smoke and the heat has become unbearable.

I hear the ominous sound of the roof collapsing inward in a nearby room and know that time has run out for us. I blindly rush down the stairs with her body cradled against mine, but the seconds suddenly seem like hours. It feels as if I'm moving in slow motion, slogging through quicksand as I make it to the bottom of the stairs.

Blinded by the heavy smoke, my trained eyes catch the slight variance of light coming from the open doorway leading outside. I crawl toward it, but my heart constricts in fear when I hear the deafening crack of timber above my head.

I watch with dread as burning plaster falls from the ceiling in large chunks around us. The intensity of the heat is unbearable, and I know we are about to die.

With a herculean strength born of terror and adrenaline, I throw her tiny body toward the light just as the ceiling collapses above me, engulfing me in flames...

I wake up screaming with my heart pounding hard in my chest.

Dazed, I hear Avery's muffled voice calling to me. She sounds as if she's miles away when she cries, "What's wrong, Lance?"

Gasping for air, I struggle to recover from the terrifying nightmare—but I cannot answer her.

Stubborn Lass

Avery

In my dream, I'm walking through a field of wildflowers, my hands drifting over their fragile blooms. But I am ripped out of my pleasant slumber by an earth-shattering scream. I immediately turn on the lamp to find Lance lying in bed, drenched in sweat, and gasping for breath.

Even though his eyes are open, I can tell he isn't here with me.

"What's wrong, Lance?"

He doesn't respond to my voice. He's still lost in whatever nightmare has him in its grip.

Placing my hand on his chest, I tell him, "Lance, it's just a dream."

It takes him several moments to recover, but then I hear his breath slow and become more relaxed. He finally turns his head and I see the tortured look in his eyes.

"I'm sorry," he whispers in a gruff voice.

I cuddle up next to him and feel his muscles still trembling. "There's no reason to apologize."

He attempts to disengage from my embrace, telling me, "You shouldn't touch me. I'm all sweaty."

"It's okay…" I hold Lance even tighter. The terror of his dream still radiates in the room and I whisper, "You're safe with me."

He shudders in my arms and a tear slowly falls down his cheek. Even though I have no idea what his nightmare was about, tears prick my own eyes in response to his pain.

I lie with Lance, my head on his chest, and listen to his heartbeat slowly returning to a normal, steady heartbeat.

"I shouldn't have stayed," he mutters, trying to break our embrace again.

Holding him tighter, I insist, "I'm glad you stayed. I would have been hurt if you'd left."

Wiping his eyes self-consciously, he glances away from me. "I hate having you see me cry like a baby."

I cradle his strong jaw in my hand and gently force him to look at me. "There's no shame in tears. Your fear was so intense that I could feel it. What were you dreaming about?"

He opens his mouth to answer, then closes it again. Pausing for a moment, he answers, "I've only told one other person. Not even my brothers know the details of the dream."

Full of sympathy for him, I assure Lance, "I don't want you to share it if it makes you uncomfortable."

He frowns slightly, shaking his head. "That's just it. I *want* to tell you, but I have no idea why."

Seeing the depth of pain in his eyes, I tell him, "When I find myself in situations like this, I recommend following your gut."

He lets out a ragged sigh, then nods to himself as if he's made a decision. Turning to me, he shares, "I've had the same fucking nightmare since I was a child. And, all through the years…" His voice catches and he pauses for several seconds before continuing. "…the ending has never changed."

"What happens?" I ask quietly.

His voice is ragged when he answers me. "It always begins with a house engulfed in flames. I hear the desperate cries of a mother begging for someone to save her child. I don't even give it a second thought, and rush into the burning building, my lungs choking from the billowing smoke. When I reach the top of the stairs, I call out to the child and hear the little girl's terrified cries. The fire is more intense upstairs, so I have to crawl into the bedroom. I find her hiding in the closet and grab her hand…"

He stops, his eyes tearing up again. I notice that his breathing is becoming more labored as he retells it. I wait patiently for Lance to continue, realizing he is vividly reliving the nightmare.

Lance's voice is ripe with pain when he tells me, "We are only feet from escape…and I hear that terrifying crack above my head." Lances closes his eyes and whispers hoarsely, "I throw the little girl toward the door just as the ceiling collapses and I am consumed by the flames."

He takes in a deep breath, shuddering violently as if he can feel the scorching heat of the fire.

I swallow hard, shaken by his dream. "I can't imagine how terrifying that is, especially when you've had to relive it over and over."

With his eyes still shut, Lance nods.

Needing to be closer to him, I snuggle up to Lance again and lay my head back on his chest. I wrap my arms around him protectively.

After several minutes of silence, he tells me in a choked voice, "There's a secret I've kept to myself about the nightmare. I haven't shared it with a soul—not even my dad.

I hold my breath as a sense of foreboding washes over me. "What is it?"

"Oh hell…" Lance lets out an agonized sigh. "I'm almost afraid to voice it out loud."

I wait quietly, my head moving up and down with his every breath.

"I know with unshakable certainty that I am meant to save that little girl I keep seeing in my dreams. I don't know when or where, but there will come a day that our paths will cross."

Goosebumps rise on my skin, and I lift my head to meet his gaze. "That's a terrifying thought."

He gazes into my eyes. "I'm prepared to do whatever it takes to save that little girl."

I look at him in disbelief. "Even if it means your own death?"

He nods. "If it comes to that. I'm sure you can't understand this, Avery, but my mother died to protect me. I've always felt as if I'm living on borrowed time."

Tears spring to my eyes hearing his confession. "No, Lance! You are meant to live a long and happy life."

Lying there in a state of shock, I lay my head back on his chest and close my eyes, clinging to the sound of his steady heartbeat.

Lance wraps his arms around me. "I'm sorry, Avery. I didn't mean for the conversation to get so dark."

I'm touched that he's been so open with me. "I'm honored that you shared your secret with me. No one should have to carry such heavy thoughts alone."

"Here's some more honesty for you, then," he states, squeezing me tighter. "I'm jealous that my brothers knew my mother…because I've had to grow up on other people's memories of her."

My bottom lip trembles and I feel his pain all over again. "That's incredibly sad."

"Good or bad, it's all I will ever know." He turns to glance at the clock and gently lifts me off his chest. Getting out of bed, he mutters, "I'd better leave before someone catches me here and the local rumor mill starts up."

I stare at Lance in concern. He dresses quickly and heads to the door, stopping for a moment to return to me. Kissing me lightly on the forehead, he smiles. "I wouldn't trade our time tonight for the world."

"Me, too." I return his smile, but my heart aches when he heads out the door and shuts it quietly behind him.

Turning off the light, I snuggle back under the covers, but the cabin feels distinctly empty now.

In the span of one night, I not only became acquainted with Lance's passionate side, but I also caught a glimpse into the tortured man behind his big personality.

I can't imagine losing one of my parents, especially in that way. My life would have been radically different without my father and mother raising me. However, I understand the heavy guilt he still carries because of her death.

It's something I can relate to.

The sound of an invisible train barreling toward me shatters the silence in the room. I press my hands to my ears, forcing back the memory.

Gavin arrives in a beat-up jeep at exactly ten the next morning. While I deeply appreciate his punctuality, I'm a little dubious when I see the condition of the vehicle he's driving.

Lance exits the jeep and walks up to me with an easy grin as if the terror of last night never happened. "You can still bow out, you know."

I scoff. "Why would I want to do that?"

He leans in close, his voice full of concern, "If you thought the lift was a challenge, Trapper's Way is a thousand times worse."

I laugh. "A thousand times worse? I think you are exaggerating. My whole problem with the chairlift was the fact that I was dangling in the air. I'm going to be in a vehicle on solid ground this time."

I look at Gavin and smile. "And I'll be with an experienced driver who knows the road. Besides, I made it down the lift by myself just fine," I claim, even though I'm exaggerating the truth just a bit.

The look of concern he had for me last night returns to his eyes. "Seriously, Avery, there's no shame in being afraid of heights. I didn't want to mention it in front of my brothers because you hadn't shared it with them yourself. But you have nothing to prove to me—or anyone."

"While I appreciate your concern, I know what I'm doing." I whip out my vial of essential oils and a pack of gum and smile at him. Striding up to the old jeep, I pat the beast and ask Gavin, "Does she have a name?"

With a twinkle in his eyes, the bear of a man tells me, "She sure does. Meet Spitfire."

"Otherwise known as 'Junker' to the rest of us," Lance teases.

Gavin gives Lance the side-eye and explains, "What my brother is referring to is the fact that I found her in a junkyard. As soon as I saw Spitfire, I knew we were meant to be. I reached out to my network of junk dealers and was able to secure all of the parts I needed to bring her back to life."

"Spitfire is a perfect name for her," I agree and begin to climb into the back seat.

"Since this is your first time, I insist you sit in the front," Gavin tells me. "It's the best view."

I glance at Lance, who shakes his head ever so slightly. While I appreciate his protective nature, I know what

I'm doing. Being in the front seat will help make me feel more in control.

Up for the challenge, I slip into the front seat, buckle myself in, and smile at Lance as he climbs into the back.

"So, how long of a drive is Trapper's Way?" I ask Gavin as he pulls out of the parking lot.

"Only seven miles. It's an old mining road through Wolverine Basin and has a bunch of switchbacks on the flank of Mount Emmons." He grins. "I'm telling you, it's the most beautiful drive you'll ever see. Lance, Finn, and I go up every year after all of the tourists leave for the season just so we can relive the experience."

"I'm excited," I tell him, turning my head and giving Lance a confident smile. I want him to know he doesn't need to worry about me.

Initially enthusiastic about the drive, my nerves start to kick in when we turn down a narrow, bumpy road made of crushed rock and lined with a scattering of large boulders. I can hear the child-like excitement in Gavin's voice when he tells me, "You're about to see some spectacular views."

I sit back in my seat, still feeling confident even as I pop some gum into my mouth and take a sniff of the oil on my wrist. We start to climb higher up the narrow road, and my tension eases when tall pine trees begin to line the road on both sides like a barrier. It's beautiful, like a mountain fairy tale.

It isn't until there is a break in the trees that I get a real sense of just how high we are. Even though my heart is racing, I remind myself that I am on solid ground as we bounce around on the rocky mountain road.

Gavin is forced to slow down several times to maneuver around larger rocks blocking our path. He winks at me, obviously enjoying the challenge of the drive.

I feel Lance's hand on my shoulder. "How are you doing?"

I turn to him, planting a smile on my face. But my voice is a higher octave than normal when I answer, "Just fine."

He squeezes my shoulder before sitting back in his seat. Although I am stubbornly resolute about continuing, I appreciate his obvious concern.

There comes a point when I grab the handle above me and hold on for dear life when I see the terrifying drop-off on my side of the vehicle. I can't even let go of the handle to get another piece of gum. So, I keep silently repeating to myself, *I am conquering my fear of heights.*

I am no longer able to enjoy the beautiful vista as we continue up the steep switchbacks. But, just when I didn't think it could get any worse, Gavin is forced to slow to a crawl as he carefully navigates around a missing portion of the road that has fallen down the side of the mountain.

"Don't worry, Miss Snow," he assures me with an easy grin. "Spitfire was made for this kind of challenge."

I swallow hard, feeling the lump in my throat grow. Knowing there is no way to turn around on this narrow road, I have no choice but to survive this.

Despite Gavin's confidence, I start shaking like a leaf and close my eyes tightly. My brother's terrified expression suddenly flashes in my mind, and I have to bite my lip to stop myself from screaming when memories of what happened come flooding back.

"Stop the jeep!" I hear Lance order from the backseat.

Gavin immediately stops and turns off the engine.

I feel Lance's comforting touch as he reaches for me. "Avery, I want you to crawl into the back with me."

"I can't," I whimper, too terrified to move.

Lance's voice is commanding but kind. "Open your eyes and look at me."

I slowly turn my head and open my eyes, meeting his gaze.

"Unbuckle her," he tells Gavin.

When I'm free, Lance grasps my hand firmly and pulls me into the backseat, where he wraps me in a protective embrace.

I melt into his arms and close my eyes again, blocking everything else out. The overwhelming sense of safety he offers, mixed with his masculine scent, washes over me like a soothing balm.

I slowly regain my composure and eventually stop shaking.

Opening my eyes, I am overcome with immense gratitude. The tender look I see in Lance's eyes stirs something deep in my soul.

"Let us know when you're ready to continue," he tells me in a comforting tone.

Sheepishly, I look over my shoulder at Gavin, who is sitting in the driver's seat looking profoundly distressed. "I'm sorry, Miss Snow."

"No, this is all my fault," I tell him. Burying my head

in Lance's chest, I feel ashamed when I confess to him, "I was too proud to tell you I'm deathly afraid of heights."

Gavin snorts. "Today was meant to be an adventure for you, not a horror show."

A burst of nervous laughter escapes my lips and I hug Lance even tighter. Although I am too afraid to look out the windows of the vehicle, I tell him, "You were right about it being beautiful up here."

Gavin chuckles uneasily, unsure what to say, and silence follows.

I peek up at him from the safety of Lance's arms and catch him staring at Lance with open concern.

"She'll be fine, brother," Lance assures him. "Give her a moment. I'll help her get buckled up in the backseat so we can proceed."

By feeling safe in Lance's arms, I avert the panic attack wanting to consume me. When I feel I'm calm enough to continue the drive, Lance sets me down in the seat beside him. My hands tremble as I try and fail to buckle myself up.

I'm relieved when Lance takes over and clicks the buckle into place. Checking to make sure I'm secure, he grabs my hand and holds it tightly.

I squeeze his hand in gratitude and nod to Gavin to let him know I'm ready to continue.

Turning the jeep back on, Gavin continues up the challenge of Trappers Way until he finds a spot where he can safely turn around. I can't describe the flood of relief I feel the moment I know we are headed back down the mountain.

I even brave a few glances out the window to take in the unique beauty of the rocky peaks. Although I feel like a fool for being so stubborn and ruining this outing for them, I'm deeply grateful for Gavin's expert driving skills.

I cannot describe the relief I feel when we finally drive up to my cabin. But I find I'm too unsteady on my feet to walk when Lance helps me out of the jeep. "Let me help you," he says reassuringly as he swoops me into his arms and carries me to the cabin.

Gavin sticks his head out of the jeep window. "Can I get you anything, Miss Snow?"

I turn my head and smile wearily. "I'm good, thank you."

Gavin then addresses Lance. "Want me to wait for you, brother?"

Lance waves his hand, gesturing for Gavin to head out. "I'll stick with Avery for a bit."

He nods, then frowns when he meets my eyes again. "I'm really sorry for scaring you."

I laugh, feeling painfully embarrassed about the whole thing. "Don't worry about it, Gavin. I give you permission to tease me about this later—just not today."

I hear his warm laughter as he drives away.

With a playful smirk, Lance asks, "Do you want to go hang gliding tomorrow?"

I smack his chest even though I'm grateful for his sense of humor.

Lance sets me down and unlocks the door, opening it wide. I escape into the safety of the cabin, and immediately collapse on the large bed, groaning loudly.

After several minutes, I look up at Lance feeling a deep sense of guilt. "I'm sorry."

He chuckles. "For what?"

"You tried to warn me about the drive, but I refused to listen to you," I growl in frustration at myself. "I'm such an idiot."

He sits on the bed beside me. "You're not an idiot, Avery. But you are a *seriously* stubborn lass."

I chuckle sadly as I stare up at the ceiling. "You know, I've never had to face my fear of heights until I came to Crested Butte…"

We sit there in silence, but the weight of it becomes unbearable when my brother's terrified face suddenly flashes in my mind. I shake my head violently, trying to hold back the memory.

"Are you okay?"

"No…"

The memory of that day has been buried for so long, but that horrifying moment lives inside me and is as clear to me as if it were yesterday—even though I was just a small child.

It is my greatest shame and regret.

I brave a look at Lance and smile sadly. "I'm a mess."

"Would you like to be alone, Avery?"

I close my eyes to hold back the tears. "No. I need you."

I feel the mattress move as Lance stands up, then hear him turn on the water for the tub.

"I find whenever I'm extremely stressed, a hot bath can soothe the tortured soul," he tells me.

I nod, feeling myself starting to relax a little just listening to the stream of hot water pouring into the tub.

I open my eyes and ask him, "How are you feeling after last night?"

He glances back at me with a guilty smile. "I know after the scare you just had, I shouldn't say this…but I'm feeling hot and bothered right now."

His answer boosts my fragile ego, but I'm concerned about him and press, "What about the secret you shared with me yesterday? Do you regret telling me?"

Lance turns off the water and leans against the tub. "It actually helped to say it out loud, and I thank you for that. It won't stop the nightmares, but I feel less anxious."

Getting the answer I needed, I know what I have to do. "I'm glad to hear that because I also have a secret that I need to voice out loud."

Lance gestures to the tub and smiles. "Why don't you undress, and I'll wash your hair while you tell me."

Even though that sounds wonderful, I'm reluctant to take him up on his offer. I can already feel my heart starting to race because I know how incredibly difficult this will be.

I sit up and glance at the tub. "How did you know I can't resist a hot bath?"

He winks and holds out his hand to me.

I quickly remove my clothes before I can second guess myself. Taking his hand, I slip into the hot water.

Despite the warmth of the bath, my body begins to shiver uncontrollably.

Like Lance, the terrible secret I keep is something I have never breathed to a living soul—not even my brother.

All In

Lance

Although I am completely distracted by Avery's naked body when she first gets into the tub, the moment I feel her trembling, my concern for her well-being overshadows everything else.

My only mission is to help her relax.

I rub the tight muscles in her shoulders and murmur, "I can feel the tension in your body." When she remains silent, I assure her, "I want you to know that no matter what you share, your secret will be safe with me."

"I trust you," she whispers in a frightened voice.

When I feel her tense up again, I pick up the pitcher I grabbed from the kitchenette and fill it with the hot bath water. "Tilt your head back for me," I murmur in a low, even tone.

As I pour the warm water over her strawberry curls, Avery moans in gratitude. The gentle sound of the water splashing back into the tub seems to soothe her and she soon begins to relax again.

When I start massaging the lavender shampoo into her hair, Avery finally speaks. "I was ten when it happened." She hesitates for a moment as if she's having second thoughts.

I don't react and continue massaging her scalp while she builds up her courage.

"I told my parents I was going outside to play that day, but I really wanted to explore outside our neighborhood. When Jake started following me, I told him to stay behind. But even at seven, he was as stubborn as me and refused to listen."

Avery shakes her head and I momentarily stop, listening to her remorseful laugh. "My mom and dad had no idea how far we traveled from our house that day."

Laying her head back against the edge of the tub, I start massaging the shampoo into her hair while she continues. "We came across an abandoned greenhouse, and we threw rocks at it. It was addicting listening to the glass break."

She turns for a moment to look up at me. "I felt so fearless that when the two of us came across a convenience store, I walked right inside with my little brother and played an old arcade game until I ran out of change."

Avery sighs and says nothing for a bit. I wonder what is going through her mind. When she lies back again, I continue working the lather through her curls. Her tone becomes lighter when she tells me, "I'll never forget how exciting it was. There were no limits on where we could go that day." She adds in a wistful tone, "I felt like I owned the world."

Her countenance suddenly changes.

"Until we came across the railroad bridge…"

A shiver goes down my spine as Avery slips her head under the soapy water and lies still for several seconds at the bottom of the tub. I have the sense that she is building up her courage, so I do nothing but wait.

She suddenly pops her head back up. I hand her a wash towel so she can wipe the soapy water from her eyes, and fill the pitcher again.

Letting the towel fall to the floor, her tone is quiet and sad, "When I saw that train bridge supported by a wooden jungle gym, I thought it was the coolest thing I'd ever seen. It spanned across a shallow ditch, connecting us to the other side. The bridge seemed like a magic portal to me, giving us a whole new place to explore!"

Avery pauses for a moment. "But when I told Jake we were crossing it, he said he was too scared."

Her voice starts to trail off as she mutters in a monotone, "But nothing was going to stop me. So, I shouted at my little brother, calling him a big baby, and ordered him to stay where he was while I crossed the bridge by myself."

She stares off as if she is watching it play out on a distant wall. "It's strange because I remember feeling zero fear when I looked down at the ditch below as I balanced between each railway tie. It was actually exhilarating to me."

In a far-off voice, Avery tells me, "Jake cried for me to come back, but when I refused, he started across. I went back to help him as we slowly made our way across the bridge. And by the time we were halfway, I had my brother laughing with my wild guesses on the magical things we would discover on the other side."

The heavy weight of her next words seemed to steal the air from the room. "That's when the bridge started to vibrate…"

I feel her shudder. I'm so close to Avery in that moment that my heart races as if I'm connected directly to her fear. "At first, I had no idea what it meant. But then I saw the train racing toward us in the distance. I screamed for Jake to run—I even grabbed his hand, trying to help him across—but he was too little and slipped between one of the railway ties."

She lets out a strangled sob. I feel her pull away from me emotionally as she connects to that terrifying memory, reliving it again.

Avery's voice becomes small as she recounts the events as if they were happening in real time. "I tighten my grip on his hand to keep Jake from falling…then we both hear the train whistle blare and I see the color completely drain from my brother's face…"

I feel the small hairs rise on the back of my neck.

With her breath coming in short, rapid gasps, she whimpers. "I can't hold onto him any longer…" Her bottom lip trembles. "He's staring up at me with terror in his eyes when I lose his grip…"

I imagine Avery's horror as she watches her brother fall.

"I'll never forget seeing his body hit the ground. It haunts me to this day."

She remains silent for a moment.

"I turn to stare at the train, frozen in place when it

reaches the bridge, blasting its whistle over and over again." Avery puts her hands to her ears, wincing as she rocks back and forth.

"I don't remember jumping off the bridge…" She slowly lowers her hands, staring straight ahead as tears stream down her face. "But it wasn't until after the train passed that I heard Jake crying."

Avery becomes withdrawn and I feel the darkness of that memory suffocating her.

I immediately stand up and grab a towel. Pulling her into my arms, I wrap her in its warmth, crushing her against my chest.

"He almost died that day because of me…" she chokes out.

"But he didn't, Avery. You both survived."

She hugs me tighter, breaking into fresh sobs. "But it was my fault, Lance! He wouldn't have been walking on the bridge if I hadn't been so stubborn."

I swallow down the lump growing in my throat, fully understanding the guilt she carries. I remind her, "You were just a kid."

She looks up at me with tear-stained eyes and says in the barest whisper, "So was he…"

I lift Avery, pressing her body against mine and gently rock her as she cries. I find it cathartic to mourn our shattered childhoods together. We were both innocents bound by profound guilt to tragedies we can never change.

Carrying Avery to the bed, I lie down beside her and finish drying her skin while she stares at me in silence. The guilt she still carries is clearly written on her face.

"Jake wouldn't have been there if it wasn't for me…and he paid the price."

I look at her with an overwhelming sense of sympathy. "The fact that you and your brother are good friends is proof he doesn't hold the incident against you."

"But he should, Lance."

I furrow my brow, realizing by the grave tone in her voice that there's more she hasn't told me. "What do you mean, Avery?"

My mouth goes dry when she tells me, "Jake hurt his leg in the fall. To protect me, he told my parents that he fell out of a tree." Avery bursts out in a heart-wrenching sob. "His right leg was permanently damaged by that fall."

I hold her close as she releases a torrent of tears, grieving for her brother's disability. When her tears finally cease, we lay there in silence together. With her wet cheek pressed against my chest, Avery whispers hoarsely, "Jake and I never talked about what happened after that day. It became the ugly secret I've kept buried deep in my heart."

"Oh, Avery…" I murmur in compassion. I understand the impact of that accident on both her and her brother on a personal level.

Fresh tears fill her eyes. "It was all my fault."

I hold Avery closer. "I understand why you've allowed this guilt to consume you." I pull back to look into her eyes so she will hear the truth. "But you were ten, Avery. You were too young to understand the danger you were in."

Her bottom lip trembles again, and she says in a broken voice, "I'm the one who should have suffered for my mistake, not my little brother. I can't tell you how many times I've wished I could trade places with Jake."

I gaze into her pale blue eyes, sharing her pain. "I've often wished I had died in the fire and not my mother. It would have saved my father and brothers from so much pain."

Avery sits up. "No, you're wrong! Your family would have suffered either way. I'm grateful your mother saved you." She buries her head against my chest and holds me tight. "Promise me you won't ever say that again."

I close my eyes, unsure if I can keep that promise. I have been wishing for that most of my life.

When Avery pulls away, she looks me directly in the eyes. "Promise me, Lance!"

Seeing how earnest she is, I concede, but tell her, "I will on one condition."

Avery looks at me warily. "What?"

"Talk to your brother."

I see her swallow hard. I realize that she finds it equally difficult to make that promise. But she finally nods, saying quietly, "I will."

In all my life, I don't think I have ever felt so seen by another person.

The "L" word floats on the tip of my tongue, but I don't want to ruin this moment by voicing it out loud.

Still…I need her to know how deeply she matters to me. I smile as I twirl a lock of her hair around my finger. "I care about you."

Her eyes soften, and a timid smile plays on her lips. "I care about you, too."

To be so raw and honest leaves us both feeling emotionally exposed, and in that vulnerability, we bond even closer. What begins as an affectionate embrace soon becomes something more passionate as I run my hands over her bare shoulders.

Avery loses the towel and wraps her arms around the back of my neck, kissing me deeply. Her tongue teases me, while her hands begin their own exploration.

"I want to undress you," she whispers in my ear. "I need to be close to you."

My cock hardens while she takes her time unbuttoning my flannel shirt, exposing my chest to the air. Running her hands over my muscles, she purrs sensually. Then she moves to my jeans and undoes the button. With a wicked smile, she slowly unzips it before slipping her hand under the waistband of my boxers to feel my hardening cock.

I hold my breath as she slides her fingers over my rigid shaft. Looking at me hungrily, she repositions herself between my legs and opens my jeans. I groan as I watch Avery take my cock in her hand and begin to stroke it slowly.

Her firm grasp ignites the inferno inside me. When she sees my precome on the head of my cock, she leans down and takes a lick.

I almost climax right then.

Gritting my teeth, I tell her, "You'll need to be careful, woman. I'm about to explode."

Her eyes twinkle mischievously. "I like that you're so desperate for me."

Avery pulls down my jeans and boxers, freeing my

cock so that she has full access to it. She then opens her mouth wide and I watch in captivated silence as she encases my shaft with her pink lips.

"Damn…" I groan, throwing my head back. As much as I love the feel of her tongue flicking the head of my cock and her warm lips going up and down my shaft, it takes colossal concentration on my part not to come.

I curl my fist in her hair and slow her movements down on my shaft so I can enjoy her mouth a little longer. "That's it," I murmur gruffly. "Nice and slow…"

The naughty girl looks up at me with those luminous eyes with my cock in her mouth, and I grunt because I'm about to lose it again. She will never understand the level of self-control I must employ not to come in that sexy mouth of hers.

When I can take no more, I pull away. "I want you, Avery."

Her eyes widen as she quickly changes position, laying down on the bed and spreading her legs to me.

Oh, God…

I know as I settle between her legs that I am about to lose my heart to this woman if I make love to her. But I can't stop myself no matter how much it might hurt later.

I reach over and grab my jeans, pulling out the square packet. Ripping it open, I quickly cover my shaft with the condom. Positioning myself above her, I stare into Avery's eyes.

"Kiss me, Lance."

Pressing my cock against her pussy, I lower myself to kiss her and hear her sharp intake of breath as our lips connect and the head of my shaft breaches her opening. I groan as my shaft is enveloped by her warmth at the same time I plunder her mouth with my tongue.

"Yes…" she moans excitedly, grabbing my ass as I thrust into her deeper.

The tightness of her pussy makes it nearly impossible not to give into my building orgasm. To keep from coming, I nibble her neck to distract me.

Again, the desire to tell her I love her rises to the surface as I revel in our primal connection. Looking down at Avery, I chose a different word when I tell her, "I have never wanted anyone as much as I want you."

In response, she wraps her legs around my waist and matches her movements with my thrusts. Lifting her head, she then whispers in my ear, "Devour me, Lance."

I spend the next hour loving Avery with my hands, lips, and tongue as I explore every part of her body. I take great pleasure in making her orgasm multiple times, holding off my own climax until I've thoroughly made love to her.

When I can no longer hold back my orgasm, I finally allow myself to release deep inside her. Never in my life have I felt so powerful or vulnerable with another person.

As I lay beside Avery, panting after the intense climax, I know with certainty that when it comes to loving Avery…

I'm all in.

Flirting with Forever

Avery

I spend my final days in Crested Butte practically living at the library while Lance works his forty-eight-hour shift at the fire station. I find the stairs do not have the same power over me that they once did, and I claim that as a solid victory. It gives me the freedom to fully explore every nook and cranny of the old schoolhouse from top to bottom.

Knowing that I'm heading back to Wichita soon, I soak in as much local color as I possibly can. While sitting on the main level, I observe a session of Story Time with a handful of preschool children when the entrance door bursts open.

An older man walks into the building struggling to carry a tall stack of boxes. I hurry from my seat and grab the top two, which look like they are about to topple to the floor.

"Thanks, miss," he says in a hushed voice, setting the

remaining boxes on the counter. Glancing at the children listening attentively to the volunteer reading the humorous picture book, *The Monster at the End of This Book*, I see the gentleman smile, showing gaps in his teeth.

Turning to face me, he quickly pulls off the knitted beanie on his head, revealing a disheveled mop of gray hair. "I appreciate the help."

I whisper back, "You're more than welcome." I glance back at the children and smile as they squeal in delight at the surprise ending of the story.

The old man nods, a pleased look on his wrinkled face. "Those tots are lucky. The one regret I have is never learning how to read."

I look at him with compassion, unable to imagine how difficult it must be to navigate everyday life without such an integral skill.

He says in a reflective tone, "All those letters remain a mystery to me…but then, I never really applied myself in school."

"Mr. Zeigler, what a pleasure to see you this morning," Flora Elwood whispers as she walks up and pats his hand. "Thank you for bringing all of the supplies we need for our festival booth."

"My pleasure, ma'am," he replies in a low voice. "I best be going. I've got a lot more deliveries to make for the Fall Festival."

As I watch the jovial man leave, I'm overcome with a sense of sadness knowing I will never see Mr. Zeigler again once I leave. For some reason, the idea of it hurts my heart.

"Is everything all right, Miss Snow?" Flora whispers

to me.

I simply nod, keeping my conflicting emotions to myself. My phone pings, and I check to see a text from Lance.

Hey, I just finished cleaning the toilets at the firehouse and thought of you.

I raise my eyebrows in amusement, causing Flora to ask, "Is anything wrong?"

I smirk, glancing back at his text. "I'm not sure…"

I see Lance in the middle of texting again.

Fact is, it doesn't matter what I'm doing, I'm always thinking about you.

I'm touched by his text but, before I can reply, he starts typing again.

So…I wanted to ask

He suddenly stops texting and my heart begins to race as I wait for him to finish.

I'm off tomorrow. Would you like to have a home-cooked dinner with my father?

I slowly let out the breath I didn't know I was holding.

"I need to answer this," I whisper to Flora, excusing myself. I head outside to give myself a few minutes to compose my thoughts before I text him back.

Standing in the bright sunshine, I stare up at the majestic peak overlooking the mountain town. There's now a crispness in the air that denotes the changing of the seasons.

It's almost time for me to go…

Although I'm excited to head home, there's a part of me that has fallen in love with this little town, and I feel sad about the prospect of leaving.

I look down at my phone and text my answer to Lance.

It would be lovely to meet your father before I go.
Great!

I giggle when I add:

I would offer to bring a dish, but we both know I can't cook.

He is quick to reply.

As my guest, the only thing required from you is your appetite.

I feel light-headed reading back over his texts. Having dinner with Lance's father feels like a big deal. Although I'm nervous about meeting him, I'm also grateful for the opportunity. It would be a shame to leave this place without meeting the man who raised Lance and his four brothers.

That evening, I spend far too long deciding what to wear. It seems humorous to me since I don't normally obsess over clothes. But the truth is, I hope to impress Lance's dad. I deeply admire the man for raising five sons on his own after losing his wife in such a tragic way.

So, I stare at the outfits I brought for the trip and vacillate between being practical by dressing for the cold night air or going all out with a classy black dress and heels—the one elegant outfit I brought "just in case".

Lance insists on picking me up for our "dinner date", even though I offered to drive to his father's place. Being punctual to a fault, I stand outside my cabin and wait for him. When he's late, I start glancing at my watch, counting each minute that ticks by.

After fifteen excruciating minutes, I decide I've been patient long enough and reach for my phone to text him. But before I can type the first word, I hear the familiar rumble of his truck.

I smile at him as he pulls up to the cabin. I hurry to open the passenger door, but he lowers the window and tells me, "Wait right there!"

Jumping out of the truck, he walks around the front of the vehicle. I notice he is holding a giant bouquet of wildflowers in a vase tied with a big satin bow. However, that's not what makes my jaw drop.

Lance Macallan is in formal Scottish dress, with a plaid vest of blue and green and a matching kilt complete with the fur pouch I know is called a sporran. He holds out the bouquet of flowers. "For you—a rainbow of wildflowers to remind you to visit this place in July."

I eagerly take the vase from him, touched by the beautiful gift and the thought behind it. However, I can't help looking him up and down in appreciation.

"I must say, Mr. Macallan, you look mighty fine in that kilt."

"I was hoping to impress you."

"Well, you most certainly have."

When I meet his gaze, I am touched by the open adoration in his eyes. "You look absolutely stunning, Avery."

I glance down at my black dress, silently applauding myself for picking the right outfit for this evening. "Thanks."

Admiring the impressive bouquet in my hands, I notice a small envelope tucked in with the flowers. "Would you like me to read it now?"

He smiles charmingly. "I want you to read it after you head out for Wichita in the morning. Let me put the flowers in your cabin before we leave."

As he takes the vase from my hands, Lance explains, "The flowers are the whole reason I'm late tonight. It was important to me that you got them before you leave."

My smile falters as soon as he turns away. It hits me that leaving tomorrow is going to be much more difficult than I anticipated.

I watch Lance return after putting the vase in the cabin and admire just how sexy he looks in a kilt. I've always fantasized about Scottish men—especially after reading one of my favorite historical romance series, *Outlander*—but I never thought I'd actually get to go on a date with one.

Our drive to the Macallan homestead is unusually quiet. There is a nervous energy between us that hasn't been there before. Time is running out for the two of us, and we both know it.

Lance turns down a long dirt road of rolling fields that leads to a tree-lined path. The bumpy gravel road leads to a modern-looking two-story cabin sporting manicured gardens in the front. The home is truly breathtaking and not at all what I was expecting.

I have to laugh at myself because I just assumed Lance's family home would match the weathered look of the Punny Peaks Motel.

Lance insists on opening the car door for me and holds out his hand, helping me out of the truck. It's something I appreciate tonight since I don't walk in high heels very often, and never on gravel.

Straightening my skirt, I follow Lance up the porch steps. Above the front door, I notice an unusual sign. The wood has been blackened, which makes the hand-carved letters stand out: "*Mo Chridhe.*"

A Scottish phrase I know means "My Heart."

The simple sign is charming and adds a special touch to the modern home.

Opening the door, Lance gestures for me to step inside ahead of him. Before I do, however, I take a deep breath to bolster my confidence.

As I pass through the doorway, Lance murmurs, "He's going to love you."

I glance up at Lance, and he winks at me.

I walk into the home, surprised when I see a distinguished-looking gentleman with a well-trimmed, salt-and-pepper beard standing in the room, along with all four of Lance's brothers.

Every one of the men is dressed in his tartan, just like Lance. I have never seen anything as swoon-worthy as the Macallan men dressed in kilts.

Lance walks up beside me, placing his hand on the small of my back as he formally introduces me to his father. "Avery, this is my father, Leith Macallan."

He then addresses his father. "This is Avery Snow, Da. The woman I've been telling you about."

I immediately notice that his father has the same charming smile as he does when Mr. Macallan holds out his hand to me. "Miss Snow, 'tis a pleasure. Ma boy Lance has only kind things to say 'bout you."

I love the sound of his Scottish accent and return his easy smile as I shake his hand. "Thank you, Mr. Macallan."

He nods, then gives Lance a wink.

I feel as if I've successfully passed the first test. However, I'm curious as to why all of the brothers are here and turn to Lance. "You didn't tell me that your whole family would be here tonight."

His father explains, "Ma sons gather here for a meal every month to remember their mam, Miss Snow. Tonight just happens to coincide with Lance's invitation to ye."

Although I feel a little foolish, I'm too curious not to ask, "Do you normally dress in your kilts for the occasion?"

"Aye," he answers. "We do it in honor of Annie Macallan."

I nod, touched by his answer.

The one brother I have yet to meet walks up to me and holds out his hand. "Good evening, Miss Snow, I'm Malcolm."

Malcolm is taller than Lance and has a classically handsome but rugged look that would be at home on the cover of any Scottish romance novel. The careful, cultured way he speaks is a bit stiffer than the other brothers. It makes sense since Clara mentioned he was a banker.

Leaning in as we shake hands, Malcolm says in a hushed voice obviously meant for his brother to hear, "I suspect my little brother is hoping to make a favorable impression on you tonight by inviting you to this particular event."

I turn to Lance and give him a thumbs up. "Favorable impression has been made."

Lance smirks, saying gallantly, "I aim to please."

I'm startled by the sound of a horse neighing so loudly it sounds as if it's standing in the next room.

Mr. Macallan chuckles. "That would be Ciarán, Miss Snow. He's the sixth son no one talks about."

Curious, I walk with Lance's father into the kitchen. When we enter the large room, I break out in giggles when I see a coal-black horse with a long mane standing at the back door. His head is sticking inside the kitchen through the top half of a Dutch door.

As soon as the horse sees us, he lifts his head and paws repeatedly at the back door as if he's anxious to walk inside to join us.

"I suspected Ciarán might take a shine to you." Mr. Macallan smiles warmly at me. "He has an eye for comely women."

I blush at his compliment and tentatively hold my hand out to the horse. Ciarán nuzzles my palm with his soft upper lip. "How long have you had him?"

Mr. Macallan gazes tenderly at the horse as he pats his black coat. "Over twenty years now, lass. He was a colt when my wife passed, and he just naturally became one of the boys."

"I hope you're hungry!" Bram announces, pulling out a large, beautifully roasted chicken from the oven.

"Oh wait, I forgot something!" Lance exclaims. He then winks at me, promising, "I'll be right back."

Lance leaves me alone in the kitchen as he rushes out

of the room. Mr. Macallan takes the opportunity to escort me to the table and pulls out a chair. "You get the place of honor as our guest."

I thank him as he pushes the chair in for me. Mr. Macallan takes his seat at the head of the table, stating with pride, "Every dish you see came directly from our land."

I look over the many dishes, amazed that nothing came from a grocery store. Coming from the city, it seems unreal to me.

Lance quickly returns carrying a square tin in his hand. He sets it on the table in front of me. The colorful tin has a picture of a rainbow-colored bull with long strands of hair like a Komondor pup I once saw.

"What's this?" I ask him, intrigued by the box.

He looks at his father sheepishly before answering. "Normally, we each make a dish for our monthly gathering, but since my shift ended yesterday, I bought this whiskey fudge instead."

I look at the tin with increased interest, curious what whiskey fudge tastes like.

"Tell the truth, brother," Bram teases. "You didn't make anything because you had *other* things on your mind."

Lance stares directly at me without an ounce of shame and answers with an alluring grin, "*Aye,* true enough."

After all of the brothers sit down at the table, I notice the chair directly opposite of me is empty even though it has a place setting. My heart aches when I realize it's set in honor of their mother.

The room grows quiet. When I notice Lance bow his head beside me, I immediately follow his example.

Mr. Macallan's low voice fills the room. "Almighty God, we come together to celebrate the bounty You have provided our family. We are grateful for Your blessings as we gather here to honor Annie, my beautiful wife and mother to these five upstanding men."

I almost say "Amen" but Mr. Macallan continues and I blush when I hear my name. "We are grateful to have Miss Snow join us tonight and pray that You will keep her safe as she travels back home to her family. We ask You to bless this meal and this time together in Your name."

I join the others in saying a heartfelt "Amen!"

Ciarán adds a spirited neigh of his own and starts shaking his head. I watch with amusement as Gavin picks up a large carrot from a bowl on the table and tosses it.

The horse catches it in his teeth and makes a muffled sound of pleasure as he chews the carrot.

The brothers begin quickly passing the dishes as they each serve themselves. Lance gallantly offers to serve me, filling my plate with a healthy portion of every dish on the table.

During the meal, I listen to the deep timber of their voices as the brothers share what's happened over the past month. They then go on to talk about world events and then argue over whether traveling back in time would be better than traveling forward.

I notice Mr. Macallan barely touches his food as he listens to his sons, gazing at them with humble pride. It's obvious he is the silent force of strength that guides their family.

Ciarán remains at the back door during the entire meal, his ears twitching back and forth as he follows the conversation. Now and then, he stamps his foot and one of the brothers dutifully throws him something to eat.

I catch Lance staring at me and feel the butterflies start up when he gives me a private wink, looking all sexy in his Scottish attire.

"Have one of these," he tells me, opening the tin and tossing me a wrapped piece of fudge. Even though I'm not finished with my dinner yet, I eagerly unwrap the candy and pop it into my mouth. The soft fudge tastes like creamy toffee with a mellow bite of whiskey. I enjoy it so much that I ask him for another piece.

Sitting here with the Macallans, I'm suddenly overcome with a feeling of belonging. For a brief moment, I allow my mind to flirt with my heart's silent plea.

What if I stay…

A Secret Shared

Lance

I can't help but stare covertly at Avery for the entire meal. Having her radiant presence in this house feels like a breath of fresh air. She brings a vitality to our family discussion because of her unassuming, yet poignant questions as she seeks to know my family better.

I notice that Malcolm is far more animated than usual when he answers her. He even returns the favor by peppering her with questions about her family.

She beams when she tells him, "My dad owns a popular thrift shop in Wichita. My parents keep it full of inventory by visiting garage sales and the local dumps in the area." She frowns when she adds, "You wouldn't believe what people throw away. But luckily, my mom has an amazing knack for taking discarded furniture and turning it into functional art."

Avery smiles at Finn. "She's a creative soul like you, but instead of stone, she can take an old table or desk and transform it into something uniquely beautiful. She never ceases to amaze me with the treasures she creates out of 'trash.' People come from all over Kansas to buy her creations at the shop."

Avery glances at my father. "My parents' mission in life is to repurpose as many discarded items as they can rather than having them buried in a dump."

My father nods with approval. "A worthy calling."

"I'm incredibly lucky because my brother Jake helps them to run the shop. He's always keeping an eye out for books he knows I might enjoy." She leans forward, her eyes flashing with delight when she shares, "You're not going to believe this, but Jake once found a first edition copy of *A Christmas Carol* while going through a box of old books someone dropped off. The book was published in 1843!"

Her voice is full of child-like wonder when she adds, "Being able to hold a piece of literary history in my hands is an experience I will never forget."

I grin at her. "Did you keep it or sell it?"

Avery looks at me as if I'm crazy. "Neither! We donated it to Wichita's Museum of World Treasures so everyone can enjoy it."

Malcolm nods, looking at Avery with respect.

"Are you a fellow book lover?" she asks excitedly.

He clears his throat, looking strangely uncomfortable. "I…umm…dabble in poetry from time to time."

This is news to all of us, and my brothers and I stare at him in collective shock.

Our brother Malcolm the banker is a closet poet?

Finn slaps him on the shoulder. "That's *braw.*"

Malcolm gives him an awkward smile and I swear I see the guy actually blushing.

Avery smiles warmly. "I would love to read some of your work."

He shakes his head, clearly horrified by the idea. "It's just scribbles. Nothing worth reading."

The moment I see Avery open her mouth in protest, I save my brother further embarrassment by interrupting their conversation. Although I know she means well, I can tell how uncomfortable Malcolm is after just outing himself as a poet.

I quickly change the subject, having a secret motive when I ask my brothers, "Any of you going to the Fall Festival this year?"

I'm not surprised when all four shake their heads.

"Is it *that* bad?" Avery asks in surprise. "Poor Mrs. Elwood has been going on and on about her booth this year."

Finn is quick to answer. "The committee always throws a good event. However, I'm still working on my sculpture." He glances at my father. "In fact, I had to force myself to leave my studio tonight."

My father gives him an amused look.

Avery then glances at Bram, who shrugs. "I'm normally slammed in the hours leading up to the festival, so I use the downtime to clean up and take the rest of the night off."

Malcolm shrugs when Avery looks at him next, not offering any excuse.

When Avery turns to Gavin, he glances at me briefly and then smiles. "I haven't been in a couple of years, but

I'll go if you are going, Miss Snow."

Avery smiles. "I'd take you up on that offer, but I'm heading back to Wichita in the morning."

Not prepared to see Avery go just yet, I interject, "What's one more day? I'd enjoy taking you to see our Fall Festival."

She smirks but shakes her head.

Malcolm suddenly takes pity on me. "I suppose I'll go if you go."

Finn gives me a brotherly nod and ups the ante. "If the rest of you are going, I could spare a few hours, I guess."

All eyes turn to Bram. He sighs heavily but reluctantly agrees to make an appearance after he's done cleaning up.

Avery's light laughter fills the room. "Why do I get the feeling I'm being ambushed?" She looks at my brothers accusingly, then breaks out in a mischievous grin.

Looking back at me, she says, "I'll take you up on your offer on one condition."

Before I can ask what it is, she turns to my father. "Would you please join us, Mr. Macallan?"

Silence fills the room as we stare at my father. I've never seen my father attend any town gathering since I was a wee child.

He chuckles. "To be honest, I haven't been to the Fall Festival in ages." His gaze drifts to the painting of our mother on the wall. In an act of solidarity, he shocks all of us boys when he replies, "I suppose it's high time I do."

Avery looks at me with amusement and shrugs. "It seems like the Macallans don't fight fair."

I wink at her, breathing a silent sigh of relief. I know we won't be saying goodbye tonight at least.

She laughs. "I can't believe I just agreed to go to the Fall Festival tomorrow night."

"That makes two of us," my father agrees.

Standing up, he nods to me. "Son, why don't you take Avery for a walk while the rest of us clean up the kitchen?"

We all stand when she gets up from her chair.

Grateful for the chance to spend time alone, I take off my jacket and cover Avery's shoulders. "I wouldn't want you to freeze on our walk."

I escort Avery out of the house, knowing full well that we will be the topic of intense conversation while we're gone.

I don't mind. Because of them, Avery is staying for another day. That is a gift I wasn't expecting, and I plan to make the most of it.

The rising half-moon brightens the dark sky, lighting our path as we walk down the line of the property fence. I tell Avery the story behind my parents settling in Crested Butte. "My mother traveled to Scotland for the summer after she graduated from college. That's actually how my parents met. My dad told me that it was love at first sight."

I chuckle, adding, "He described it as a lightning bolt."

Avery slips her hand into mine. "That's so sweet."

Grasping it tightly, I continue, "My father said he

knew he was destined to marry her, so when it came time for her to return to the States, he proposed."

"Wow," Avery exclaims. "That's not a long courtship at all."

"No," I chuckle, feeling a sense of pride that they were so bold and unapologetically in love. "When my mother said yes, my father agreed to return to the States with her. She insisted they live somewhere that would remind him of Glencoe, the highland village he was leaving behind."

I stop and look up at the mountain peak silhouetted against the starry sky. "That's how we ended up here in Crested Butte."

"Your parents picked a beautiful spot for their homestead, even if it's in the middle of nowhere."

Squeezing her hand, I tell her, "I actually prefer it being secluded."

She laughs. "Well, I happen to like the fast pace of the city."

"And I like the stillness of nature." I grin, swinging her hand as we walk.

"You know, I'm not opposed to the quiet," she admits, stopping for a moment to look up at the stars. "It's easy to forget to slow down when you're in the city."

"I bet."

We continue walking in the pleasant silence, listening to a lone owl hoot in the far distance. Wanting to extend the evening for a little longer, I decide to share something close to my heart. "There's a special place I'd like you to see."

Avery instantly agrees. "I'd love to see it, Lance."

"My father visited this place so often that I decided when I was twelve that I was going to make a bench so he would have a proper place to sit."

She wraps her arm around my waist as we walk. "What a kind thing to do."

"Yes and no." I chuckle. "You'll know what I mean when you see it. I'm just saying—don't judge."

Avery's laughter fills the night air.

Damn, I'm going to miss that sound.

My heart literally aches with the realization that I've found my soul mate, but out of respect for her, I will stay silent when I watch her leave.

My Heart

Avery

We walk down a seldom-used road lined on both sides by groves of pine trees laced with Aspens. The road leads us to a hilltop that opens up into a spacious clearing with the tall mountain peak in the background.

It is a picturesque spot hidden away from the rest of the world.

I notice a lone bench sits near the center. As we approach it, I suddenly smile, understanding what Lance meant. The bench is patchworked, built from various pieces of wood. It's charmingly uneven, reminding me of a Picasso painting.

"I know it doesn't look like it, but it is safe to sit on," he assures me. "Just be wary of splinters."

I chuckle as I lean on the arm of the bench and then carefully sit down. He sits beside me and stares straight ahead. I listen to the soothing sound of a slight breeze playing among the pine trees. Soon, I snuggle up to him, purring. "It's peaceful here."

He slowly nods in agreement.

"So, is this where your father goes to think?"

"Nae. This is where he comes to remember."

I turn my head when I hear the hint of sadness in his voice. "What do you mean?"

He points to the open field in front of us. "In the summertime, this area becomes a field of wildflowers. It's quite remarkable…really."

I smile, imagining it, and snuggle closer to him. "It must be lovely."

"Yes…" he says in a reflective tone of voice. "It's brought our family comfort, although my brothers don't come up here often."

"Why not?" I gaze at the field surrounded by trees, moved by the quiet beauty of this hidden place.

When Lance turns his head, I see the glint of tears in his eyes. "This is where the old homestead used to be."

Goosebumps rise on my skin as understanding suddenly flows through me. I look back at the clearing. "This is where it happened…"

He nods, a painful gasp leaving his lips.

"I can't imagine how hard it must be to come here," I tell him with compassion, honored that he would share this painful part of his past with me.

Lance stares out at the clearing again. "I used to resent my father for spending so much time out here by himself. It felt like he was rejecting us boys…me…because he would stand here for hours mourning my mother."

I take his hand in mine and squeeze it.

Lance clears his throat before continuing, "News of my mother's passing rocked the community when it happened. People came from all over Gunnison County to pay their respects to my mother. But, instead of having a funeral, they came with materials and built a new house for us five boys. Fire Chief Higgins even made sure that every room had a sprinkler installed to help ease our fears."

A lump forms in my throat. I'm deeply touched by their practical compassion and choke out, "That's beautiful…"

"It was. They were able to salvage a piece of wood from the house and it sits above the front door now."

I recall the blackened sign when I entered their home, now realizing its significance.

"*Mo Chridhe*," he says, the words rolling off his tongue with a beautiful lilt. "It means 'My Heart'…the name my parents chose for their homestead."

I struggle hard not to cry.

The two of us sit in the shared silence for several minutes before he wraps his arm around me and pulls me closer. "When I was young, I would come up here to spy on my father. Back then, I was riddled with guilt because I knew I was the reason she died."

He pauses for a moment before confessing, "It wasn't until I was twelve that I realized the truth. He wasn't coming here to mourn but to remember her. This home was where they started their lives together and birthed five children. It's the only place in the world where he feels close to her."

Tears fall down my cheeks unheeded. I swear I can feel the love of his mother surrounding us as we sit.

"That was a life-changing revelation for me, Avery. So, I built my dad this bench."

I run my hand lightly over the rough wood of the homemade bench set in this field of memories, appreciating the love behind Lance's gift to his father.

He looks at me in the pale moonlight, a sad smile on his lips. "I'm going to miss you when you leave."

The love I've been trying to suppress suddenly bubbles up, and I press my lips against his, expressing my truest feelings through my kiss. When he wraps me in his arms and kisses me with equal fervor, my heart skips a beat.

I lose myself in our prolonged kiss, knowing there is no turning back now.

I love Lance Macallan.

Spurred on by those intense feelings, I ask Lance back to my cabin and we talk late into the night, pouring out our souls to one another. I want to know everything about the man down to the smallest details. The openness of our exchange leaves me breathless and excited.

At one point, Lance suddenly becomes silent and lightly brushes my cheek with his fingers. Gazing at me with those captivating seafoam eyes, he murmurs, "You are truly remarkable, Avery."

Flying on the high of our soulful conversation, I cradle his face in both of my hands and *almost* tell him what my heart has been longing to say out loud.

Instead of words, I let my lips express my love for him. The kiss that follows will forever be marked in my memory. Opening my heart and being fully accepted and cherished by this extraordinary man has changed me.

Desperate to physically express the intense emotions we share, Lance and I slowly take off our clothes and stand before each other completely naked.

It feels different tonight.

As we lay on the bed together, it seems that every kiss, every touch, is ripe with meaning. Running my hands over his muscular chest, I trace my finger over his heart and smile. "You have an incredibly sexy body, Lance Macallan."

He wraps me in his arms, pressing his naked body against mine. I feel the hardness of his shaft against my lower belly as he rolls over, positioning himself above me.

"I thought that the moment I spotted you on the side of the road without your shirt." Lightly tracing the freckles on my shoulder, he murmurs, "And I've been obsessed with these freckles ever since."

Lying beside me, Lance begins kissing my neck as his hands explore my bare skin. I bite my lip, trying not to laugh when his fingers graze the sensitive area on my stomach. It causes unbearable tickles to shudder through me.

He grins, then trails his hand lower, resting it just above my pussy. "Tonight, I am going to make passionate love to this body."

I kiss him deeply again, hungry to feel his unspoken love.

Lance takes his time as he explores my entire body, tasting and teasing me. He carefully builds up the sexual tension between us. Attentive to my needs, he discovers new erogenous zones I never knew existed and brings me to the edge multiple times!

When he's finally driven me wild beyond distraction, Lance slips on a condom and settles between my legs, positioning his cock against my pussy. I moan in anticipation, desperate for him.

And then he does something I'm not expecting…

My heart completely melts when he whispers, "I love you" as he slowly thrusts his shaft into me.

I momentarily forget to breathe when I hear him say those words. Throwing my head back, I revel in his love as he slowly thrusts into me with his thick shaft, expressing his devotion to me with the depth of each stroke.

Grabbing his muscular ass, I push him in even deeper, needing all of Lance. He increases the intensity of his thrusts, and I ride the waves of pleasure he creates with each stroke.

"Kiss me…" I beg when my thighs begin to tremble.

Lance presses his lips against mine and his thrusts also come harder and faster as he looks into my eyes. I cry out in ecstasy, experiencing the intense connection known only to lovers.

I can't stop smiling as I lay next to Lance. I never knew sex could be this fulfilling! Lance not only knows how to please my body, but I have never felt so cherished while lying in a man's arms before.

The chemistry we share is off the charts, but the tender intimacy between us is something I never believed was possible. I turn my head to stare at Lance, completely blown away by the intense feelings I have for the man.

My heart skips a beat as I gaze at his handsome face and think, *I want to wake up beside him…every morning.*

But I can't afford to think about settling down with Lance. Not only would I face the risk of losing him in the line of duty, but it also would require me to leave the support of my friends and family back home.

Still…

As I gaze into Lance's eyes, I have to fight the feeling of "home" that he inspires in me.

Being in love with the man makes the path ahead even more tangled. The doubts I harbor about making a permanent life with him still nibble at my soul, but I also can't deny the overwhelming love I feel.

Life is full of risks, right?

He must sense my inner battle because he smiles and asks, "What are you thinking about, beautiful?"

Placing my hands on his chest, I return that gorgeous smile of his. More than anything, I want to explore what a future with Lance would look like. And the only way to do that is by spending more time with him.

With my heart beating wildly in my chest, I say in a casual voice, "I'm calling Mr. Gregory on Monday about the contract."

Lance's eyes flash with interest. "Really?"

My smile grows wider when I see his reaction. "It would be an invaluable experience for me to run Old Rock for two years." I look down shyly, before meeting his gaze again. "And it gives me more time to explore *us*."

Lance shakes his head, a look of pleasant disbelief on his face. "I've been counting down the days until you head back to Wichita, certain that I would never see you again." He glances out the window at the sunrise just beginning to crest the mountain range.

"The heaviness I've felt in my chest is gone." He then smiles back at me. "It feels like everything has changed."

I nod in enthusiastic agreement. Now that I have voiced my intention to stay in Crested Butte, I have never felt so alive!

From the first day when Lance helped me save the tiny kitten, the Universe has been leaving me signs and hinting at my future here. Even though I came reluctantly to Crested Butte in search of a job, I've been embraced by this close-knit community. Then there's Lance Macallan, the man I have fallen for…despite my best efforts not to.

I know about his tragic past and the nightmares that still plague him. His courage to be vulnerable and open with me about his childhood trauma has given me insight into my own. Although I have yet to resolve what happened with Jake, it's because of Lance that I understand what I must do for my brother's sake…and mine.

I smile as I glance at *Jane Eyre* sitting on my

nightstand. I've spent my whole life experiencing love through beautiful books, and now I have the opportunity to create a love story of my own.

The emotional high that I'm on is suddenly interrupted by Lance's phone.

He reaches across the bed to grab it and then gives me an apologetic look. "It's from Chief Higgins."

I nod, understanding he must take it.

Lance quickly throws on his clothes and briefly excuses himself as he leaves the cabin to take the chief's call.

In the deafening silence that settles over the cabin, fear begins to creep in. If I'm serious about pursuing a future with a firefighter, I have to accept that this is my life now—and anything can happen at any time.

However, I would never want to change Lance Macallan. I admire him for the fearless man he is, and I'm proud that he is willing to put his life on the line to protect the people in this town. Uncertainty and risk are a part of loving this incredible man.

And I trust I'm woman enough to handle it.

Fall Festival

Lance

Standing outside Avery's cabin, I find I'm full of nervous excitement. After Avery's surprise announcement that she is staying, I have to take a deep breath before answering Chief Higgins' call.

He immediately barks, "Are you attending the Fall Festival tonight?"

I glance back at the cabin and grin. "I am. Why?"

"Unfortunately, Veronica Roberts just called in sick and we have a scheduled training early tomorrow morning for the new batch of rookies. I want to know if you can take her place."

It appears I'm back in Chief Higgins's good graces despite the now-infamous Kitten Debacle. The fact he asked me to take over is a vote of confidence in my abilities as a leader. "Absolutely, Chief. Not a problem."

"I'd advise you not to stay out late."

I chuckle, finding his parental advice humorous.

Then he throws me for a loop when he asks, "Are you okay, Macallan?"

Apparently, he can tell something is up. Unable to hide how ecstatic I am right now, I answer truthfully, "Never been better, Chief!"

I head back to the cabin and open the door to find Avery lying on the bed with a come-hither look in her eyes.

"I hope that wasn't an emergency, Mr. Firefighter," she says, rubbing her hands all over her seductive body. "Because I need someone to put out *this* fire…"

Shutting the door, I growl hungrily. "Don't worry, ma'am. I'm a professional at putting out fires."

I arrive back at the homestead at the crack of dawn—just in time to catch my dad heading out to milk the cows.

Nodding to me, he grins. "I take it things went well last night."

"Avery is taking the job," I tell him, still in shock that she's staying.

I notice the glint in his eye when he says, "Can't say I'm surprised. Ye two couldn't take yer eyes off each other last night."

Unaware I was that obvious, I chuckle self-consciously.

"I'm truly happy for ye." Placing his hand on my back, he pushes me toward the stairs. "Now go to bed 'n' get some rest."

Too hyped to sleep, I offer to help him instead. "Why don't I take over the milking for you this morning?"

He shakes his head, giving me a knowing look. "Don't be worrying about yer old man, son. Best to rest now. Take it from me, it's important not to yawn on a date."

I burst out laughing. "I'd love to hear how you learned that pearl of wisdom."

He smirks. "Another time. Now off with ye."

Knowing there's no point in arguing with my father, I head off to bed and find the kitten sleeping in the center of my pillow. After stomping several times, I resort to shaking the pillow slightly to wake her.

She looks up at me groggily and gives me an irritated meow.

Picking up the annoyed furball, I look into her sleepy dual-colored eyes, unable to contain my disbelief. "She's staying, girl!"

Setting Moonbeam back down, I quickly strip off my clothes and slide under the cold blankets. She immediately crawls back onto the pillow, smothering my face with her soft fur as she gets comfortable.

Blowing her fur from my lips, I murmur, "You do realize that without you, this would never have happened."

Moonbeam purrs in response.

I snort, still reeling from the fact that I said "I love you" to Avery. I've spent my entire life avoiding commitment, and yet, here I am…

I love her. I love her more than the air I breathe. I

rub the ache in my chest, not wanting Avery to ever regret getting involved with me.

Right there in bed, I make a vow to God, promising to do everything in my power to keep myself and my team safe whenever we respond to an emergency call. I'm determined not to crush Avery's heart the way my father's was when he lost my mother in the fire.

Concerned that my nightmare might return if I fall asleep, I stare up at the ceiling. However, the kitten's soft purr has a powerful calming effect that carries me into a deep slumber devoid of dreams.

I don't wake until noon but, to make up for it, I spend the day helping my dad do routine maintenance on all of the farm equipment in preparation for winter. When it's time to pick up Avery to take her to the fall festivities, I jump in my truck, tired but also elated.

Pulling up to her cabin, I'm struck by the fact that Avery would be gone if she had stayed with her original plan and left this morning for her trip back to Wichita.

Instead, she pops her head out of the door and points to her phone.

I nod in acknowledgment. Seeing the serious expression on her face, I realize she must be talking to her parents. I'm curious how they are handling the news that she is signing the two-year contract at Old Rock.

A few minutes later she comes bounding up to the truck and jumps in. "How goes it?" I ask nonchalantly as she buckles up.

She glances at me apprehensively. "Naturally, my family is surprised to hear I'm not driving back this morning, but they're supportive of my decision to take the job." She looks down, fumbling with the seatbelt.

"And how are you feeling about it?" I press lightly, wondering if she is having second thoughts.

Avery looks up and smiles. "Honestly? I'm happier than I've ever been."

I lean over to kiss her. "I feel exactly the same."

On the short drive to the park, Avery laments, "I can't believe the price of places up here. Now that I plan to stay, I'm going to have to seriously hunt for an affordable studio apartment in town."

"The cost of housing has gotten ridiculous. At the time my parents bought their property, Crested Butte was just a blip on the map, and the land was affordable. But they bought it a few years before the ski resort was built and changed all that."

I smirk when I tell her, "It's part of the reason I still live at my father's place. I pay 'rent' by helping my dad with the farm whenever he needs it."

Avery nods. "I would do the same if my family lived here." Looking at me quizzically, she asks, "If you're a full-time fireman and work part-time at the motel, do you mind me asking what you do with all that money since you don't pay rent?"

I shrug. "Since I don't need much, I let Malcolm manage my money. He's the President of the local credit union and a genius when it comes to investments."

She sits back in the seat and stares out the window. "You're smart to do that. I live beneath my means so I can put a small nest egg set aside, but I don't want to use it to supplement rent. I sure hope I can find something affordable here."

"Don't worry. Malcolm has connections with the rental owners who bank with him. I'm sure he'll be able to provide you with people to contact."

"Good." She sighs in relief. "Because I wasn't having much luck searching the web."

I chuckle at her naivety. "Most rentals here never get listed because they're snatched up as soon as they become available."

She grins. "Then I'm lucky I've got connections."

I'm surprised to find a parking spot on the street directly across from the city park. As I pull in, Avery asks, "Do you think any of your brothers are already here?"

"Possibly, if Gran roped one of them into helping her set up her booth. But Bram usually closes the diner and cleans up once the festival starts. And it's a safe bet that Malc will make a brief appearance before heading back to his office."

"Ah…"

Out of habit, I grab my N94 face mask from the glove box before getting out of the truck.

"What that's for?" Avery laughs as she watches me slip the mask into my pocket.

I shrug when I answer. "It's something I saw Chief do my first year as a firefighter whenever he attends a large gathering while off duty. Seemed like a prudent thing to do in case there's a fire, so I've done it ever since."

I see her glance nervously at my pocket, but she chooses not to say anything. While I understand that the mask may make her uncomfortable because it's a reminder of my profession, I like having it with me.

It acts as a safety net. Although I've never needed it, simply knowing I have it makes me feel more at ease.

I take Avery's hand and squeeze it as we walk under the colorfully decorated Fall Festival archway as we enter the park. I know that the townsfolk are bound to notice Avery is still here and I figure if tongues are going to wag, I might as well give them something extra juicy to gossip about.

I point out the small hay bale maze on the other side of the park. It has been a staple at the festival ever since it began, and it remains a favorite with families as well as couples.

One of our local bands is already strumming tunes on the pavilion, which the social committee spent hours decorating with fall foliage and pumpkins. A handful of couples are already under the tent they set up, dancing to the music.

As I lead Avery to the complimentary bar set up outside, she teases me. "Going straight for the alcohol?" Leaning in, she whispers, "There's no need. I'm all yours tonight."

She has no idea how her words affect me...

Subtly shifting my jeans, I lean against the counter. "We'd both like a Gaelic Punch," I inform Salvatore, the gifted Italian mixologist who runs the outdoor bar every year.

Avery raises an eyebrow. "Well, isn't that a fun name for a drink?"

"Wait until you taste it," I tell her. "This drink will warm you inside *and* out."

Avery rubs her hands together excitedly as Sal pours the hot drink into recyclable cups and garnishes each with a lemon slice studded with cloves.

After stuffing my tip into a plastic pumpkin on the bar, I hand Avery the drink.

She purrs as she holds the hot cup. "My fingers already thank you."

I wrap an arm around her, saying in a low voice, "Maybe you can run those warm fingers over me…"

She winks before taking a sip. Her eyes widen in pleasure when she tastes the sweetened Scotch and fresh nutmeg. "Yum…this is seriously delicious!"

Holding up my cup, I toast, "Here's to our first official date."

She clinks her cup against mine. "And a night we won't forget."

As we walk down the row of carnival booths, Avery stops at the booth with Balloon Darts. "I loved this game as a kid."

Mr. Zeigler, who is manning the booth this evening, immediately smiles the moment she walks up. "This is an unexpected surprise, Miss Snow."

Avery graces him with a radiant smile. "It's wonderful to see you again, Mr. Zeigler."

"Welcome to our Fall Festival. Would you like to play?" He holds out three darts to her. "All donations go toward the Animal Welfare Society."

"I sure would!" Grabbing the darts, Avery hands him ten dollars before taking a wide stance as she eyes the balloons.

"I see you take this dart-throwing seriously," I comment with amusement.

"I certainly do, Mr. Macallan," she replies in a formal voice, keeping her gaze locked on the wall of balloons. To my astonishment, Avery pops only the purple balloons in rapid succession like a pro.

Mr. Zeigler exclaims, "That takes real skill!"

Clapping my hands in appreciation, I tell her, "I want you on my team."

Avery winks at me and then thanks Mr. Zeigler. When she starts to walk away, he beckons her to come back. "You can't forget your prize, Miss Snow."

She waves off the offer. "Oh, no, I only did it for fun."

"Skills like that deserve to be rewarded. You can have anything on the table," he states with a grand flourish as he points to the largest stuffed animal.

Avery scans her many choices but chooses a simple candy necklace. "This was my favorite as a kid."

"Are you sure?" he asks her, obviously amused by her choice.

"A hundred percent. Thank you." She slips the necklace into her coat pocket and smiles.

As we continue down the row of games, I lean in,

knocking shoulders with her. "What other mad skills do you possess that I don't know about?"

"I happen to be a cornucopia of surprises," she says, looking up at me with a teasing grin.

"I bet you are…" Leaning in to kiss her sensuous mouth, I taste the sweetness of the drink on her lips and growl.

"Aren't you worried about what people will say?" Avery murmurs as she kisses me back.

"Not in the least." To prove my point, I wrap my arm around her waist and kiss her again.

Gavin suddenly appears and taps my shoulder.

When I break our embrace to look at him, he grins. He then turns his attention to Avery. "I'm glad to see you're having a good time."

"I am," she says, glancing at me coyly.

I suddenly catch a glimpse of Malcolm behind Avery and nudge Gavin. "I can't believe our brother is trying his hand at Apple Toss."

He chuckles in amusement, rubbing his palms together. "This should be fun to watch."

Malcolm is dressed in a business suit. Only he would overdress for the festival. Knowing how bad my brother is at throwing, Gavin and I watch him as he tosses apple after apple, completely missing the bucket most of the time. The poor guy has never been athletic, preferring his studies over the outdoors.

Getting serious, he takes off his jacket and rolls up his sleeves before trying his luck again.

"Have you seen any of your other brothers?" Avery asks Gavin.

He nods toward Finn sitting on a hay bale on the other side of the park. The two of us casually make our way to the Punny Peaks Pumpkin Patch, where Finn is busy carving out an artistic rendition of Crested Butte on an extra-large pumpkin.

My gran's face lights up when she sees us. "I'm tickled to see ma boys here at the festival this year," she gushes. "It's been far too long."

"It has, Granny," I agree, giving her a kiss on the cheek.

She smiles at me, and then tells Avery, "I was so happy this morning when you said ye were staying. I *knew* ye were going to love it here, lass."

"You did say that on my very first day here," Avery laughs.

Glancing down at Finn's impressive carving, I decide to give him some brotherly advice. "You've got the angle of the peak all wrong. Better start over."

Finn slowly puts down his knife and huffs as he looks up at me, then flips me the bird.

"Oh, my *gourd*, Lance, stop giving your brother a hard time," Granny jokes with an impish gleam in her eye. "Beauty is in the *pie* of the beholder."

Avery actually chuckles at her terrible puns.

Malcolm heads toward us several minutes later. Even at a distance, he looks extremely uncomfortable as he clutches a purple bunny in his hand.

Gavin snickers when he sees it. "What's with the rabbit?"

Avery stares at Malcolm with a knowing smile. "I suspect there's a woman here that he plans to surprise with it."

I know my brother and scoff at her suggestion.

But he surprises me. Instead of joining us, Malcolm stops for a moment and scans the crowd.

My two brothers and I watch with growing interest as he walks toward a large group of women. We are not at all surprised when he loses his nerve and strolls past the ladies.

But I gape in surprise when he walks up to a lone woman. Her back is to us, but I see that she's wearing her hair in a tight bun.

By now, my brothers and I are completely invested in this little drama, thinking Malcolm is about to make his move…until he hands the stuffed animal to the little girl standing near her.

"Lost his nerve," Gavin states.

"He sure did," Finn agrees as we watch the little girl squeeze the bunny and grin up at Malcolm.

"I think that was incredibly sweet," Avery states in his defense.

I click my tongue in disappointment. "Malcolm's so wrapped up in his career that he wouldn't know what to do with a girlfriend if he ever got one."

Avery gazes intently at the little girl. "I think your bother knows exactly what he is doing…"

I look back to see the child grab the hand of the woman my brother just spoke to. When the woman turns her head as Malcolm walks away, I realize it's the new baker. She's caused quite a stir in Crested Butte because she keeps strictly to herself. I've rarely seen her outside her shop, and nobody knows anything about the woman. The fact that she's here with her daughter tonight is a bit of a shock.

I notice the smile on the woman's face as she continues to watch my brother. As for my brother, he is completely oblivious. He keeps glancing at his watch as if anxious to head back to the office as he walks over to join us.

Glancing at Avery, I laugh. "I think you give my brother too much credit."

Bram suddenly walks up beside me, grumbling, "I think there's going to be trouble tonight."

I follow his line of sight and see Killian walking up to the outside bar.

All five of us grunt in unison as we stare at the odious man.

"Something needs to be done before he causes any trouble," Bram snarls.

Avery looks at the five of us with a worried expression. "Surely, he can't still be upset about the pumpkin?"

Killian glances in my direction and glowers at me, nudging the person next to him.

Yep, it looks like there's about to be trouble.

"Avery, go check on Gran, will you?" I tell her when I see Killian slam down his drink and start walking toward me.

As my four brothers move to stand on either side of me, he saunters up unsteadily, a sneer on his face. It's obvious the man is already drunk. His malevolent demeanor causes the festival-goers nearby to become quiet and a crowd soon starts to gather around us.

"There's nothing to see here," I tell everyone.

Killian keeps his eyes fixed on me. He looks like he's itching for a brawl.

I stare the man down, wondering if I am about to discover the reason behind his intense hatred of me. Not a fighter by nature, I nevertheless ball up my fist, ready to lay the man out if necessary.

Flora Elwood comes running up from behind her booth and pleads with him. "Stop, right now, Heath Killian! There's no need for any of this. We're all here to have a good time—"

"That's right," my father answers in a firm voice, placing his hand on my shoulder. "The Macallans are not here to fight."

He moves to stand directly in front of me, then purposely turns his back on Killian.

Spreading his arms wide, he tells the five of us, "This is a festival, so let's celebrate with our friends."

The crowd's murmurs of agreement are interrupted by someone screaming, "Fire!"

I immediately turn to see black smoke rising from the middle of the hay bale maze. People start running around in a panic, desperate to put the fire out.

My brain instantly switches over to emergency mode. My extensive training allows me to block out everything not relevant to the situation. I know that hay bales burn hot but more slowly than straw, so time is on our side.

"Avery, I need you to remain here," I command.

Her bottom lip trembles when she pleads, "Lance,

please be careful!"

I shout to the crowd, "Everything is going to be okay. Just stay back!"

I tell my brothers and father to follow as I run to the maze. With adrenaline pumping through my veins, I assess the height of the hay bales stacked on the edge of the maze at six feet high, and easily launch myself on top. From that vantage point, I direct my family and the few off-duty firefighters who've joined us to start removing the bales to the left of me, creating a direct route to the center of the maze so everyone can easily escape.

Yelling at the families trapped in the maze, I point in the direction they need to head as the flames grow in intensity and smoke begins to cover a portion of the maze.

I notice movement out of the corner of my eye and see the head of someone cowering near the center of the maze. I call to them, but they do not respond.

The accumulating smoke starts to obscure my view. Although the path through the maze is swiftly being cleared and I know the emergency vehicles will be arriving soon, I understand the danger they're in.

There's no time to waste.

Pulling out my N95 mask, I look to my father when he calls to me and note his fearful expression. He realizes what I plan to do as I put the mask on, and he shakes his head in warning.

But there is no time to question, only to act.

I race across the tops of the bales to the sound of

Avery's terrified scream of "Don't go!" echoing behind me. By the time I locate the teenage boy, I see he's frozen with panic and curled up in a fetal position. I can hear the sirens of the fire engines coming as I jump down into the maze. I immediately recognize Tyler, the quarterback of our high school team.

"Tyler, you need to get up and follow me—now!"

But he remains frozen, muttering to himself unintelligibly.

With fire intensifying and the smoke billowing around us, I make the decision to pick him up in a fireman carry and slowly navigate through the maze as I head toward the escape route being carved out by the bystanders.

I hear my father call out to me from the eye-watering haze of smoke, helping to guide my path. With his help, it doesn't take long until Tyler and I are free from the burning maze.

I'm blinded by the flashing lights of the emergency vehicles as the boy's parents race up to me.

It feels as if time suddenly stands still when I lock gazes with Avery. I'm deaf to everyone rushing up to pat me on the back, congratulating me for my quick action.

Our eyes remain locked on each other as I take off my mask.

Avery has a look of sheer terror in her eyes…and my heart constricts.

I walk toward her, holding out my hand, trying to assure her that I'm okay. She runs blindly to me, her eyes filled with tears as she cries out my name.

Even though everyone escaped the maze and no one was hurt, I can tell that watching me rescue Tyler has rocked Avery on a fundamental level.

Tonight is a visceral reminder of the core fears we both face in loving each other.

Providence

Avery

After returning to the cabin, the two of us strip off our clothes and take a hot bath in the large tub, wanting to rid ourselves of the scent of smoke that lingers.

Even though my back is pressed against Lance's muscular body and his strong arms are wrapped around me, I still can't shake the memories of seeing the person I love disappear into the maze while flames reach up toward the night sky.

There's only one other time I've felt that terrified and helpless in my life.

"Are you okay?" Lance asks, gently rinsing soap off my skin.

I hesitate for a moment before answering. "I'm better now."

"But…"

I sigh, deciding to tell him the truth rather than

brushing it aside. "It seemed like I was living out the nightmare you shared in real time while I waited for you to make it back out of the burning hay bales. Even though your grandmother assured me that you were okay, I didn't believe her until I saw you emerge from the maze carrying that young man over your shoulders."

I turn my head to look back at Lance. "I was frozen in place. It wasn't until you took off your mask and held out your hand to me that I could truly breathe again."

He kisses my cheek. "I'm sorry it was frightening for you, but I was never in danger. I vow to you that I won't stop pursuing additional training, and I won't take any unnecessary risks. I will keep myself and my crew safe whenever we respond to emergency calls. However, I also will *never* hold back if I can rescue someone without causing harm to myself."

I nod, but I'm still unable to shake the terror I felt in the moment. When I close my eyes, I see him jump into the maze as I scream for him not to go. The scene suddenly changes, and I am back on the railroad bridge, listening to the whistle blare as the train barrels straight toward my brother and me...

When Lance moves my wet hair to kiss the freckles on my shoulder, I tense.

"Talk to me," he whispers.

I get out of the bathtub and grab a fluffy towel, handing one to Lance. After we dry off, I lead him to the bed and ask him to snuggle under the covers with me.

"I'm sorry. I should be your greatest cheerleader after what you did tonight. You saved that young man's life!"

He shrugs nonchalantly. "I knew what needed to be done and, with help, no one got hurt." His modest smile says everything to me. Truly, Lance is a hero in every sense of the word, and I can't help falling in love with him a little more.

"I heard from your grandmother that the young man confessed to smoking with his friends in the maze, and that's what started the fire."

Lance nods. "It seems the boys were horsing around, and Tyler dropped his cigarette in between two hay bales. When he tried to retrieve it, it got sandwiched in tighter and the hay caught on fire. When he couldn't put out the flames, he panicked instead of seeking help."

He shakes his head. "It's an all too common but deadly reaction to fire."

"Thank goodness you were there," I murmur, looking into his eyes.

He smiles. "It struck me that I wouldn't have been at the festival tonight if it hadn't been for you." He leans in and kisses me on the lips. "I take that as a good sign."

I wish I could return his smile, but I still can't shake the fear triggered by tonight's events.

He pauses for a moment before saying in a gruff voice, "I can tell you're not okay with this."

I lay back against him, tears welling up in my eyes. "It was hard, Lance."

He squeezes me in his powerful embrace. "I know. I could tell it was difficult for my father as well."

"I can only imagine…" I force back the tears when I tell him, "He is stronger than I am. To lose his wife in a fire, only to have his son choose to fight fires must take a huge toll on him.”

“He understands that I do it to honor my mother. However, I saw the fear in his eyes tonight,” Lance agrees. “Even knowing how hard it must be for him, I can’t change who I am.”

I nod. “I’m sure he wouldn’t want you to.”

“Am I too much for you, Avery?”

That question hangs in the air between us as the room grows quiet.

Not knowing the answer myself, I look at him. “Do you know what I really need right now?”

“Tell me,” he murmurs quietly.

Instead of making passionate love, I curl up against Lance and lay my head on his chest so I can listen to his constant heartbeat. We spend the evening watching an old musical, *Seven Brides for Seven Brothers,* which is playing on the television. It is a favorite movie of my mother’s and something I watched with her whenever it came on TV as a kid.

Having Lance beside me as I watch the couples fall in love and dance together is just what I need. It helps to quell my fears and I soon fall asleep, safe in his arms.

Early the next morning, I awaken to find Lance on his phone. He quickly sets it down on the nightstand and immediately gets dressed.

“Are you headed off for the training?”

He doesn’t smile when he answers. “No, there’s a fire on the other side of Whetstone Mountain. Everyone is being called in.”

Fear clutches my heart. “How bad is it?”

He keeps his voice guarded and calm when he answers. "The only precipitation we've had for the last two months was the day you and I saved Moonbeam."

Chills run down my spine on hearing his answer, and I pop quickly out of bed. I'm terrified for him and hug him tightly. "Oh, Lance…"

He gives me a reassuring kiss on the head. "Don't worry about me. I'll be safe. But I've got to leave *now*."

But I can't let go of him. I'm overwhelmed with the feeling that if I do, this might be the last time I ever see him.

"Every second counts," he reminds me, gently prying himself from my arms.

My voice catches as I look up into his eyes. "Please come back to me."

"I will." As he rushes to throw on his boots, Lance adds, "When I come back, we'll celebrate your future at Old Rock. It's going to be okay, Avery. This is what I'm trained for."

I nod, too frightened to utter a word as I watch the man I love head out the door.

Forcing my body to move, I grab my robe and hurry to the door to see him off, waving from the doorway as his red truck speeds off.

Once he's gone, a feeling of dread washes over me. I walk back into the cabin and shut the door. A part of me realizes this is his life…and maybe mine as well. In the heavy silence that follows, a vision of Lance stumbling in the forest, his body engulfed in flames, drives me to my knees, and I bawl uncontrollably.

Down the mountain, I hear the sound of the sirens from emergency vehicles heading out. They mix with the blaring of the train whistle from my childhood, and I cover my ears with shaking hands, trying desperately to block out the horrifying vision of Lance's death.

Screaming in agony, I crawl on the floor to my bed and curl into a ball. My heart starts pounding hard as a cold chill grips my entire body. I'm rendered helpless as a full-on panic attack consumes me.

Breathe! I remind myself.

Closing my eyes tightly, I force myself to take in a slow breath and hold it before letting it out slowly. I can already tell this is going to be a bad panic attack…

Hours later, I hear someone pounding on the cabin door and I bolt upright from the bed. "Lance?"

"It's me, lass," Clara calls out from the other side of the door.

I slowly get out of bed and cinch the tie of my robe before opening the door. Instantly, the smell of smoke fills my nostrils.

"Is Lance okay?" I cry in fear.

"I'm sure he is," she states firmly. Glancing toward the south, she says in a solemn voice, "I just received the official call at the office that they've issued an evacuation notice for our town due to smoke from the fire."

I follow her gaze and whimper when I see huge plumes of smoke billowing from behind a large mountain to the south. It terrifies me to know that Lance is up on that mountain peak right now fighting the blaze.

Glancing at the sun I let out a gasp. It is partially obscured by the thick smoke filling the valley, turning it an ominous deep red.

I glance once more around the cabin, hoping against hope that I've packed everything. I have never felt such a driving need to head back home.

The last twenty-four hours have been humbling.

I love Lance Macallan because of the fearless man he is. There is no greater profession than to be a firefighter. The strength of character it takes for him to willingly put his life on the line to protect the people of this town is truly awe-inspiring. And I would never ask him to step away from his profession.

But I haven't forgotten the recurring nightmare Lance has of burning in the flames. It's impossible for me to shake the sense of growing dread knowing that he's up on the mountain battling the raging forest fire. As much as I admire his bravery, I'm convinced I am going to lose him today.

The absolute terror I feel as I look at the billowing plumes of smoke on the mountain makes one thing crystal clear to me: I am incapable of being the support-ive partner he needs. Lance deserves a strong woman with an unwavering belief in him. Someone who not only understands but also appreciates the risks he takes every day to protect this community.

Because of the intense love I have for Lance, I find it devastating to realize I am not that woman.

I glance at the large vase of wildflowers sitting on the table and catch a glimpse of the small envelope tucked in the stems. Although he asked me not to read it until after

I left Crested Butte, I take it from the vase and open the tiny envelope.

> *No matter the distance that separates us,*
> *I will always love you, Avery.*
> *~Lance*

I press his note against my chest with tears streaming down my face. His declaration of love is both beautiful and heartbreaking.

I pick up the vase and run it to the car, buckling it into the passenger seat. The love infused in these flowers will provide much-needed comfort on the lonely drive home.

With my hands shaking, I write a message to Lance. I put his note to me in my pocket as I slip mine back into the tiny envelope, entrusting it to Clara before I leave.

> Please forgive me, Lance. I'm not brave enough to
> stay.
> ~Avery

Into the Fire

Lance

As I approach the fire, the sunlight filters through the smoke, making it look as if I'm on another planet. The red hue is eerily beautiful and dangerous.

We all know that the slightest wind shift can get our team in trouble. It's ingrained in us to constantly look for an escape route.

Acutely aware of my surroundings, I scan the area, noting the intensity of the fire and the direction of the wind. One simple miscalculation can put us all in jeopardy, so I continually reassess where I am and how to get out and regroup with the others if things get out of control.

Walking up close to the fire, my team and I start digging the fire line to prevent the blaze from spreading. Based on the dry conditions and the current size of the fire, experience tells me we're all in for an excruciatingly long day.

The air is already thin this high up, making it hard to breathe with the smoke whirling around. With my eyes burning and my nose running, I work diligently to clear the pine needles and dry grass to create a path the fire won't cross.

Suddenly, the winds change, and we hustle to reach the head of the fire where the clouds of ash and soot are swirling more violently. Even though the mountain air is cool, being so close to the fire, it feels like I'm sitting in an oven as I rush to create a new fire line with my team as the plants and trees crackle around me like fireworks.

The intensity of the fire creates strong gusts that blow burning embers into the air. At the same time, I hear the familiar whooshing roar each time a tree is consumed by the flames. I notice a fiery dust devil swirling soot and red embers wildly in the air as it rushes toward me.

I hold my breath and turn away before it hits my back and sputters out. Wiping any remaining embers off my turnout gear, I continue to work on the fire line.

After twelve hours on the frontline, my crew loads up and we start the drive back to the firehouse. We are completely exhausted.

But, because of our quick response, the fire is contained with the help of numerous firefighters from the surrounding counties, along with the aerial firefighting crews.

I send a quick text to Avery to let her know I'm okay.

With the smoke no longer posing a threat to our town, people line the streets to wave at us on our way to the station. There is a solemn exuberance among us when we reach the firehouse. It's a happy occasion even though we are all dog-tired and eager to head home.

I take an extra-long shower to rid myself of all of the sweat and smoke. My muscles twitch randomly, responding to the intense workout brought on by the day as I lather up my weary body. Still, I can't stop smiling while toweling off, grateful that I'll be seeing Avery soon.

Montoya walks up and bumps my shoulder. "What are you grinning about, Macallan?"

I lower my voice, "Guess which library just secured the best librarian in the country?"

"Gunnison?" he replies sarcastically.

I punch him in the arm. "You're an ass, you know that?"

"Says the donkey in the room."

We nod to each other in gratitude, thankful we've survived to fight another day.

Driving my truck down the main street, I'm surprised to see that the new bakery is still open. I make a quick stop to check on the woman Malcolm spoke to last night.

I immediately recognize the baker when I enter, because of her tight hair bun. She nods to me when I enter her shop.

"Are you and your daughter all right?"

"Yes. I drove to Gunnison with Hailey to wait until

they lifted the evacuation order so I could return as soon as possible." She looks around the bakery. "This is all I own in the world."

Wanting to support her business, I decide to buy something. "I'd like to buy one of your cakes and have you personalize it for me."

"Certainly. Which one would you like?"

Having no preference, I tell her, "Whichever one you think tastes best."

"They all do," she insists. "But I've got you covered."

I explain what I want written on the cake, giving her strict instructions not to share the news with anyone until it's officially announced.

"That won't be an issue," she assures me with a slight smile.

I realize it was unnecessary of me to ask since she keeps to herself.

I watch as she takes a round cake out of the display and writes my message in elegant writing, adding a decorative element as an afterthought. She holds up the cake for my approval, and I grin when I see the message written in her stylish script:

Congratulations

Miss Snow

Old Rock is lucky

to have you

I point to the decorative stack of books she's added to the cake. "Avery will love the extra touch. Thank you."

"My pleasure." She carefully places it into a cake box.

When she hands it to me, I'm struck by the quiet confidence I see in her eyes. To be honest, I've never really noticed her before. Thinking back to the festival, I wonder if Avery might be right about my brother Malcolm having designs on our town's new baker.

"How much do I owe you?" I ask.

"There's no charge, Mr. Macallan."

I furrow my brow. "Why?"

She states matter-of-factly, "In honor of you saving this town."

I shake my head. "It's my job. Please, how much do I owe you?"

She meets my gaze and smiles. "Your bravery helped save my shop. Consider this cake a small thank you."

When I open my mouth to protest, she holds up her hand. "As owner of this bakery, it's my prerogative."

Realizing I'm not going to win this battle, I place my hand on my chest and give her a heartfelt thank you. But as I open the door, I realize I've been remiss and turn around. "I don't think I've formally welcomed you to Crested Butte."

She nods. "I appreciate it, Mr. Macallan."

Heading straight to the motel, I immediately notice Avery's cabin is dark and her car is missing. Looking at my phone, I see that she never responded to my text.

I get out of my truck and walk straight to the office. Inside, I find Gran behind the counter.

"Do you know where Avery evacuated to?"

Gran shakes her head, but I can't miss the look of

concern in her eyes as she pulls out a small envelope and holds it up. "She instructed me to give this to you."

With trepidation, I take it from her and unfold the paper inside.

> Please forgive me, Lance. I'm not brave enough to
> stay.
> ~Avery

My stomach knots as I fold it back up and thrust it into my jacket pocket, forcing back my emotions.

But Gran recognizes what's happened by the expression on my face. Walking from behind the counter, she places her hand on my arm and asks softly, "Is she coming back?"

I shake my head. Caught off guard by this unexpected turn of events, I feel as if my heart has been ripped from my chest.

But I understand…

Avery was already struggling because of the incident at the festival the night before, and I saw the sheer look of terror in her eyes this morning when I left to fight the mountain fire.

My job is inherently dangerous.

What sane person could risk loving someone like me?

Do grown men cry?

Hell yes, they do.

As I lay in bed that night, I'm quick to wipe away any tears that escape before they can hit the pillow. There's nothing I hate worse than a wet pillow.

Moonbeam smashes the top of her head against my jaw and starts purring.

I know she is trying to be a comfort, but she's so closely tied to Avery that she acts as a painful reminder of what I've just lost.

I'm not brave enough to stay…

I can sense the pain Avery suffered while writing those words. Because I knew our relationship was doomed from the start, confessing my feelings to her was the wrong move. I should have stuck to the plan of letting her go and keeping my feelings to myself.

But I knew when I made love to Avery that first time that I was a lost soul. I will never love anyone else. And now, she's gone.

The air has been sucked out of my lungs and I find it difficult to breathe.

I hear a ping on my phone and pick it up out of habit, but my heart begins to race when I see Avery's text.

I'm so grateful you're okay!

I am. Did you make it back to Wichita?

No. I drove so slowly over the mountains that I got a ticket and just made it to the border of Colorado. I'm staying overnight here in Burlington.

Wanting to keep the conversation light, I text back:

I've never been there. How is it?

Small. Very small.

Then I might like it.

She texts a laughing emoji.

I wait as she continues to text.

I'm sorry, Lance. I suffered a bad panic attack after you walked out the door. As soon as you left the cabin, I had visions of you dying on that mountain. It wasn't until I saw your text tonight that I could really breathe again.

I assure you I'm fine. Although it was rough going, we had other crews join us to fight the fire. No structures were damaged, and no one was hurt.

She takes a while to respond.

Can you forgive me?

I close my eyes. Knowing she's gone for good crushes me, but I respond:

There's nothing to forgive. You and I are in an impossible situation. I meant what I said in the note.

Although we are separated by hundreds of miles, I know she is crying.

I'm sorry, Lance. You deserve better than me.

I answer Avery truthfully, certain that if she had stayed, she would continue to panic every time I went out on an emergency call.

I want you to be happy, Avery.

She immediately answers back.

I want the same for you.

Emotionally exhausted by the extreme highs and lows of the last two days, I end our conversation.

Good night and sweet dreams, Avery.

I can't stop the intense love I feel for this woman. As I set the phone down, I find the impossibility of our relationship almost humorous.

Having never felt this exhausted before, I pet the

purring kitten on my chest until I fall asleep.

The house is engulfed in fire…but something is very different.

When the mother cries out, begging for someone to save her young child, not another soul is around.

Realizing I am the only person who can rescue the child, I rush blindly into the burning house and choke on the thick, black smoke.

Forcing my way up the stairs, I find the second story eerily quiet except for the terrified cries of the child nearby.

I'm forced to crawl on my hands and knees because of the intensity of the heat. With painful tears blinding my eyes, I make my way to the bedroom.

I feel it in my bones that I'm too late and am about to die in this coffin of a house as the fire rages around me. But I continue forward despite it, undeterred from my mission.

I call out and am relieved when I hear the child's frightened cries. "I'm here now," I respond even as the heat of the air burns my lungs.

Ripping open the closet door, relief floods my soul when I feel the desperate grasp of the child's tiny hand.

"It's going to be okay…"

Incredible power surges through my muscles as I make my way back down the stairs with the child clutching me tightly.

Hell, in all of its fury, cannot stop me.

The intensity of the fire has increased tenfold by the time I reach the main floor. I gaze up at the ceiling in fear and see the flames dancing above me in waves like a fiery river.

The sight is both spectacular and horrifying, and, for a moment, it captivates me.

Clutching the child tight against me, I blindly lunge in the direction of the front door and our only escape. I hear a deafening crack of the timber right above my head and watch in horror as pieces of burning plaster start falling from the ceiling.

The heat has become unbearable, and I hear the toddler's terrified cries of pain and fear.

Time suddenly stands still as I gaze down at the child and realize…

The child in my arms is me.

With herculean strength born of sacrificial love, I throw the little boy toward the door as I scream out in glorious victory.

I wake up in the dark, covered in sweat, my chest heaving as a strange peace washes over me.

Lying there in the silence that follows, a new understanding begins to flood my thoughts. All these years, I assumed the dream was about me saving the little girl.

But I was wrong.

The haunting dream of my death wasn't about me…it was about my mother's fearless sacrifice when she saved me from the flames.

Instead of horror and sadness, I am filled with overwhelming gratitude and a sense of hope.

I get up and quickly throw my clothes on. Leaving the warmth of the house, I walk up the road to the hidden glen in the darkness of predawn.

Sitting down on the bench I built with my own hands, I look out over the empty field.

Instead of sorrow, my heart is full of appreciation. The heavy weight of believing I'm living on borrowed time has been lifted off of my chest.

I shout out loud to my mother so she can hear my grateful cry, "Thank you for saving my life!"

When I hear an owl hoot in the distance, I smile to myself.

Perspective changes everything.

Keeping a Promise

Avery

I keep glancing at the vase of flowers buckled in my passenger seat as I drive the final few miles to Wichita. Completely drained emotionally and physically, I unlock the door to my apartment and immediately collapse onto my bed.

But as I lay there in my bedroom, I'm startled to find that it doesn't feel like home anymore.

The last two weeks have changed my entire perspective.

I glance at my phone, encouraged by Lance's texts to me last night. He will never know how much his kind response means to me.

I can trust Lance on a level I've never been able to trust anyone.

When he said "I love you," it wasn't an impulse, it was his truth. Although I've never said the words back to him, in every caress and kiss, I returned that love.

Lance is a part of me now. But it leaves me in uncharted waters.

Sadly, nothing has changed here in Wichita. I'm still a librarian without a library. However, staying in Crested Butte isn't an option anymore. The thought of losing Lance absolutely paralyzes me, and there is no way I could ever stay away from him if I took the job at Old Rock.

For now, I only have one viable option—though it's something I never wanted to do. With a heavy heart, I grab my laptop, set it on my chest as I lay on the bed, and begin applying as a substitute librarian at the different public libraries in the city.

Instead of being in charge of a library, I will be doing basic circulation duties like shelving and pulling items to fulfill holds. Since I'll be working at multiple branches, I'll have to adjust to each library's layout and policies without being able to build any real rapport with the staff or patrons there.

This feels like a huge step down in my career, but it is the only way to keep a job related to what I love until I can find something permanent.

Unfortunately, as a substitute, my hours will not only be inconsistent but well under forty hours. Unable to live on that kind of money, I plan to take advantage of my parents' longstanding offer to help my brother manage their thrift shop.

Later that afternoon, Jake swings by my apartment uninvited and pounds on the door. "Open up! Your little brother needs coffee."

I hurry to the door and watch silently as he makes his

way over to my kitchen table using his cane. The over-whelming guilt that washes over me acts as a catalyst. Whether I am ready or not, the time has come for me to keep the promise I gave Lance.

With my back turned to Jake, I make a fresh pot and mutter, "There's something I need to talk to you about."

"I'm listening," he answers good-naturedly.

"Give me a minute."

My heart beats faster as I stare at the coffee pot slowly dripping into the carafe, trying desperately to build up my courage. Once the coffee is brewed, I carry two coffee mugs to the table and slide one over to him.

Sitting down beside him, I remain quiet as I watch him slowly stir the pumpkin spice creamer that he likes into his coffee.

I realize now that pumpkins will always remind me of Crested Butte.

Jake glances up and frowns. "This must be serious."

I'm so nervous about the conversation ahead that I can't meet his gaze when I answer. "It is."

He slowly sets down his spoon and asks with concern, "What's this about? Did something bad happen in Crested Butte?"

I swallow hard and shake my head. I wonder if dredging up the past might ruin the close relationship I have with my brother. Jake has been my best friend since we were little, and I would be gutted if this discussion changes that.

"Avery, you're starting to freak me out."

Letting out an anxious sigh, I stare down at my cup of coffee when I tell him, "Remember that day we've never talked about?"

When he doesn't respond, I glance up to see his face has lost all color.

I almost lose my nerve…but I know he needs closure as much as I do. Even if my brother ends our friendship today, I owe him that.

Steeling myself for the worst, I tell him, "The time has come to talk about it, Jake."

He shakes his head. "The past is the past. Let's leave it there."

My bottom lip trembles when I confess, "I can't."

We sit in silence staring at each other, both of us afraid to speak.

Jake finally picks up his cup and takes a long, noisy sip. I notice his hands are trembling when he sets it back down.

Seeing my brother's physical reaction instantly transports me back to that moment. As the ominous sound of the train whistle announces our impending doom, I suddenly lose his grip when he slips between the railway ties.

I swallow down the huge lump in my throat as I glance at his cane. "I never meant to hurt you, Jake."

"It was fucking terrifying, Ave."

My voice quivers. "It was…and it's been eating me up inside ever since." Unable to hold it in any longer, I suddenly cry out, "It's all my fault!" A torrent of tears follows as I relive the horror of seeing his terrified expression as he fell.

When I look up, I can't read his face.

Is this the moment I lose him forever?

Jake groans, covering his eyes with his hands. "Don't say that."

I hold my breath, prepared for my brother to unleash his justified anger on me.

Instead, Jake grabs my hands, squeezing them painfully tight. "The accident was my fault."

"No!" I shout vehemently. "I was the one who wanted to cross the damn bridge."

"You told me not to follow you. You even said it before you left the neighborhood, but I refused to listen to you. There was nothing you could have done to keep me from following you that day."

I look at him with compassion. "Don't you dare blame yourself. You were just a little kid."

"So were you, Ave."

I glance at his cane again, overcome with remorse. "But your leg…"

Jake growls in disgust as he stares at his leg. "You would have made it across the bridge if you hadn't had to help me. You would have been fine on your own, but I refused to be left behind." His eyes get a far-off look. Finally, he chokes out. "I'm still haunted by that train whistle."

I nod, hearing it echo in my mind.

"It hammers in my head constantly, reminding me of how fucking close I came to watching you die."

It's eerie to me how our silent torment has mirrored each other's all these years.

"I don't even remember how I made it off the bridge," I confess.

He looks directly into my eyes. "You jumped off it

like you were Spiderman, landing only a few feet from me. You immediately covered my body with yours when the train thundered past."

Jake's expression changes. "The bridge rattled violently, and the train kept blasting its fucking whistle as it passed over us. I'll never forget that sound. It went on forever and wouldn't stop!"

I can hear the pain in his voice and scoot my chair closer, so I can hug him while he relives the terror of that moment.

"After the train left…I couldn't stop crying. Do you remember?"

I look at him sadly and shake my head.

"Well, I do. You dried my tears with the bottom of your shirt and insisted on carrying me on your back all the way home. When Mom saw us and asked me what happened, I knew we would get in serious trouble, so I lied about falling out of a tree."

Mortified, I tell him, "I should have spoken up, but I was too ashamed. I'm sorry, Jake."

"Why? It wouldn't have done any good to tell our parents," he insists. "And it's not as if we ever did it again."

I look at him sadly. "I made a vow to make it up to you. I promised God that I would do *anything* to protect you…" I glance down at his leg, adding in a broken voice, "…even if it was from me."

Jake's eyes brim with tears. "I've never once blamed you, Ave. Not once."

"But I ruined your life."

Pulling away, he frowns. "What are you talking

about?"

"You had to drop out of soccer. Who knows? You might have been the next Landon Donovan."

Jake scoffs. "Are you forgetting the last time I played? I made a goal for the other team. I was never soccer star material."

I choke out, "But you might have been."

He laughs, wiping away the remaining tears in his eyes. "You can let that one go, sis."

But I can't! I look at him in concern, wishing there was something I could do to make up for the pain I've caused him.

Leaning forward, he asks me, "You know what I *do* miss?"

"What?" I hold my breath as I wait for his reply.

"Your fearlessness. You were the bravest person I ever knew. No one was as cool as my big sister."

I swallow hard. "Not anymore."

"I'm ashamed to say I thought that, too…until you headed to the Rocky Mountains in search of a job. For a woman terrified of heights, that was seriously a badass thing to do."

"Stupid is a better word," I mutter.

"No, it was inspiring, Ave. Seriously."

A comfortable silence settles over us as we stare at each other.

He finally breaks the silence by saying, "I'm actually glad we talked…even though I feel completely drained right now and am in need of another cup of coffee."

I nod in agreement, picking up his cup to refill it. "I guess Lance was right. This was exactly what we both needed."

Jake looks startled. "You talked to him about what happened?"

"I did," I answer frankly, as I pour us both a fresh cup. "We actually shared a lot of personal things while I was there."

I think back on that particular conversation and add, "He made me promise to talk to you because he said it would help."

I set the full cup down next to him and sit.

Jake looks at me in disbelief. "I'm shocked you shared it with anyone."

"I love him, Jake."

I glance down at my cup after making that confession and sigh. "However, I never told him that."

Jake stares at me intently. "Why?"

I look up to meet Jake's inquiring gaze. "Because he's a firefighter and I'm afraid he might die on an emergency call." Looking away I add, "I'm not brave enough to take that risk."

He snorts. "Whether you told him or not, if you are in love with him, then you've already taken the risk."

I close my eyes as Jake's words sink in, realizing he's right.

"Damn…"

Cat-alyst for Change

Lance

"What's with the cake in the fridge?" my father asks after I head downstairs and walk into the kitchen.

Having already told him about Avery after I returned from the fire last night, I let out a weary sigh. "You taught me not to waste food, so I brought the damn thing home."

"In that case…" He takes out the cake and cuts a big slice, putting it on a plate. He then starts to cut another.

"None for me," I mutter irritably.

He pauses mid-slice. "It's a travesty to waste food."

I roll my eyes. "Fine."

Cutting an even bigger slice, he carries them both to the table and slides the plate toward me. "This should help take the edge off."

"Nothing can do that," I grumble. I half-heartedly slice a small piece with my fork. My dad nods as he watches me take a bite. I'm not expecting it to taste amazing and mutter in surprise, "Wow…"

He smirks. "Incredible, isn't it? I snuck a taste earlier."

I take a bigger forkful of cake, suddenly appreciating how talented our new baker truly is.

"A forkful of happiness in every bite." My father grins, staring at the cake. "Good thing Bram isn't a baker, or she would give him a run for his money."

I nod in agreement.

While we finish our cake, my father asks in a more serious tone of voice, "Once the fire is completely neutralized, what are your plans?"

"I want to take advantage of the lack of precipitation if the weather holds and go hang gliding on Crested Butte."

He gives me a thoughtful look. "You've always found that sport relaxing."

"Aye, and I'm desperate for some time outside of my head."

"Have you ever thought about leaving?"

I furrow my brow. "Here? Of course not."

He says nothing, and takes another large bite, chewing it slowly. "A parent's job is to build a foundation for their children—not a prison."

I look at him strangely. "What do you mean by that?"

He states in a solemn tone, "There's no reason to worry about your old dad, son." Having said that, he gets up from the table and sets his plate in the sink before heading out the back door.

I hear Ciarán neigh from the pasture in greeting as I sit there alone at the table in stunned silence.

I'm unsure how to interpret the odd conversation.

Gavin drives me up the mountain on the old service road. I'm grateful for his silent presence as I assemble the hang glider.

Even though I've done this countless times before, I walk toward the launch site, my heart racing with excitement as I hold onto the bar of the glider.

It's a perfect day to go gliding. The air is crisp and the skies are clear.

While I hook and lock my harness to the center of the glider, Gavin calls out behind me, "I'll meet you down below."

"I plan to be a while," I warn him, wanting to ride the thermals for as long as I can.

"No worries, brother," he assures me. "Take all the time you need."

"Thanks!"

I'm grateful Gavin understands and doesn't pry by asking questions about Avery.

Taking a deep breath, I relax my fingers and grip the frame more lightly. I start running toward the edge, knowing that once I start, there's no turning back.

I run off the edge of the steep cliff and the glider starts to lift as my feet leave the ground. Quickly positioning my legs in the pod harness, I'm now free to fly like a bird.

There is no other experience like it.

Hang gliding is far superior to jumping out of an airplane because of how incredibly quiet it is when you soar high above the ground. It is the closest thing to the feeling of flying that I experience in my dreams.

For a time, I lose myself in the dramatic silence.

Gazing down on the small town of Crested Butte far below me, I break into a smile. This is the place I've lived my whole life. I'm familiar with every building and with the people who work and live down there.

I hear my father's low voice play in my head as I recall our brief conversation this morning. "A parent's job is to build a foundation for their children—not a prison…"

I've never thought of Crested Butte as a prison. This town is not only my community but also part of my identity and livelihood. It is a living, breathing extension of me.

Why would I ever consider leaving it?

Then it hits me. I would leave this place for Avery, just as my father left Scotland to be with my mother.

That realization flies like an arrow straight to my heart. All this time, I've placed the ball firmly in Avery's court when I am an equal participant in our relationship.

Her need to be close to family may be the very solution to our problem.

My father's quiet wisdom during our discussion over cake went straight over my head…until now. Because, the moment I consider the possibility, I can see myself moving to Wichita so Avery can lean on the support of her family.

It might be the key to unlocking our impossible situation.

It's possible that, with her parents' support, Avery might be able to conquer her fears about my profession so we can pursue a life together.

I look up to see a pair of eagles circling above. Leaning to the left, I soon catch the thermal they are on and quickly rise. The elation I feel as I soar with the birds adds to my excitement as I contemplate our possible future.

However, there is one major hurdle that stands in my way.

Once I get back to the farm, I immediately head to the barn. I need my father's guidance, and it only takes a few simple words from him to help me see things straight.

"Do ye love her, son?"

"Aye!"

"Then what are ye still doing here?"

"What about the farm? I've experienced for myself the amount of work it takes to maintain it. How will you get along without help?"

"Like I told ye before, there's no reason to worry over yer old man. I'm capable of hiring help whenever I need it."

"And Granny's motel?"

He chuckles. "She can hire another worker, ma boy. You are free to follow your own path."

For the first time in my life, I realize the barriers holding me back from leaving this town never existed. "That's it then."

"Aye." My father nods. He pats Ciarán on the neck with a pleased look on his face.

It's amazing how the trajectory of your life can change in the blink of an eye. Wanting to surprise Avery with a visit, I book a flight to Wichita and look up her father's shop online to find the address.

As luck would have it, Avery's brother answers when I call to make sure I have the right shop.

It's obvious that Jake is suspicious of me based on his tone, but I appreciate his straightforwardness and his obvious devotion to his sister. When I explain my intention to surprise Avery with a visit, he agrees to pick me up from the airport. I suspect he wants to check me out before I see her, but I don't mind. I have four brothers of my own and know how protective they can be.

He ends our call, saying, "I believe seeing you will bring my sister much-needed clarity."

I glance at Moonbeam after I hang up. Based on the last thing he shared, I get the impression Avery might be struggling. I immediately call the airlines and tell them I will be bringing my cat with me on the plane. I don't mind the extra cost. Although I've grown used to my little feline companion, I'm happy to give her up if Avery needs her.

The simple fact is that Moonbeam is as much Avery's as she is mine.

I stand outside the thrift shop, holding Moonbeam in a cat carrier, while Jake goes inside alone. I've come dressed in my Crested Butte field uniform—the same uniform I wore the day we shared a kiss on the chairlift.

Wanting to have a little fun, I tell Jake to ask his sister to go to the backroom to price items while he offers to man the cash register.

I wait five minutes before entering the shop to ensure Avery is busy pricing items. Quietly moving to the back of the store, I release Moonbeam and nudge her toward the entrance of the backroom. As soon as the kitten spots Avery, she makes a beeline straight to her.

I struggle not to laugh when I hear Avery screech in fear before crying out, "Oh, Moonbeam, is that you?"

Standing behind a tall piece of furniture, I watch covertly as Avery emerges from the back cradling the kitten in her arms while looking around the store for me.

Several of the shoppers glance in my direction with amused smiles on their faces but are careful not to expose my location to her.

I hear Avery call out to Jake. "Have you seen the man that belongs to this kitten?"

"I have no idea what you're talking about, sis."

While he's speaking to her, I walk up behind Avery and say in a low voice, "Maybe I can assist you."

She turns and her whole face lights up when she sees me.

I stare into her pale blue eyes and am rendered speechless for a moment.

"I can't believe you're here, Lance!"

I smirk. "I thought it was only fair that I should visit your big city."

Wrapping her arms around my waist, she stands on tiptoes to give me a kiss. The moment our lips connect, the world ceases to exist. It's just Avery, me, and the kitten between us.

I hear the people in the shop break out in applause, and I pull away.

Avery turns to the shoppers and smiles shyly. She then looks to Jake and says in an accusing tone, "You knew about this and didn't say anything to me?"

He just shrugs with a huge grin on his face.

Turning her attention back to me, Avery asks in a breathless whisper, "What are you really doing here?"

I cradle her cheek in my hand and smile. "Moonbeam and I missed you."

Avery presses herself against me when I kiss her again, and we both feel Moonbeam squirm between us.

Jake comes to the rescue, holding his arms out to Avery. "Let me take the poor kitten before someone gets hurt."

I notice the pink hue on her cheeks when she hands Moonbeam over to him.

The moment I see the kitten has been safely transferred, I sweep Avery into my arms and start carrying her toward the entrance of the store. The small crowd of shoppers erupts into cheers as I kick open the door and carry her outside.

"You're crazy!" Avery laughs in delight.

I kiss her possessively, not caring who sees it. "It's true. I'm crazy about you, Avery."

Three Little Words

Avery

I can't help myself and keep glancing over at Lance as I drive down the highway. I still can't believe he's really here in Wichita!

Since I already had plans to watch the Chiefs football game with my parents after I finished my shift this afternoon, I make the decision not to change my plans so they can meet the man I've been talking endlessly about.

As I drive, Lance tells me, "I had an epiphany recently."

I turn my head and smile at him. "What about?"

"Because I've spent my entire life in Crested Butte, I've never *once* considered leaving it. But after you left, one thing became abundantly clear."

I look at him in concern. "What was that?"

"Although it may be an old cliché, it remains true…" His low chuckle fills my car. "Home is where the heart is."

I nod in agreement. "I've been confronted by that thought myself."

"However, it wasn't until I had a serious conversation with my dad that I realized he had the same revelation after meeting my mother."

Understanding suddenly hits me. "When he left Scotland to be with her…" Up until this moment, I never fully appreciated his father's sacrifice.

"It was a bold move on his part," Lance states. "My dad turned his world upside down to be with the woman he loved." Chuckling lightly, he adds, "Although it's not as impressive as a move across the world, I'd do the same for you."

Although I'm touched, my heart sinks a little. "I hate the thought of you leaving Crested Butte."

Lance seems unsettled by my statement and is quiet for a moment. "Are you saying that you don't want to be together?"

"Not at all!"

Knowing this conversation is far too important to have on the highway, I take the next exit and park my car on the street so I can talk to him face to face.

Turning to Lance, I smile as I gaze into his seafoam eyes. With my heart beating out of my chest, I finally say those three little words I've been scared to voice, "I love you."

Lance stares back at me in surprise as a slow smile spreads across his face.

I nod as I watch the truth of my feelings sink in for him, and repeat with unrestrained passion, "I love you,

Lance Macallan!"

Overcome with emotion, I fling myself at him in the tight confines of my VW Bug and shower him with kisses.

"I love you, too," he murmurs huskily, grasping the back of my neck as he returns my amorous embrace.

"All I want is a lifetime of you…" I confess.

Caught up in the moment, I unleash all that love pent up inside, and we spend the next half-hour making out like teenagers. Afterward, I straighten my hair in the rearview mirror, giggling like a flushed schoolgirl.

"You're radiant, you know that?" Lance says, staring at me intensely. "I noticed that the first time I met you at the motel."

My heart skips a beat when I turn my head and catch his tender gaze. I don't think I have ever felt so adored.

I can't stop smiling as I start the car and get back on the highway. Wanting my parents to be as surprised as I was, I knock on their door and stand beside Lance on the front porch.

I smile at Lance, feeling the butterflies start as we wait for one of them to answer the door.

My father opens it cautiously, then laughs when he sees me. "Why didn't you just walk inside, Pumpkin—?"

He stops short when he notices Lance standing next to me. "Who's this?"

I tremble with excitement when I introduce him. "This is Lance, Daddy."

"Well, isn't this quite a surprise!" My father chuckles as he opens the door wider. "Please come in."

Lance insists I enter first before following me inside.

"My daughter speaks highly of you," he tells Lance as the three of us walk to the living room together.

My mother stands up from the couch with a shocked look on her face when we enter the room. Quick to recover, she greets Lance warmly when I introduce him. "Mom, this is Lance. He surprised me at the store—with help from Jake."

"It's lovely to finally meet you, Lance," my mother says, gesturing to the couch. "Please sit down."

I notice the tender look Lance gives my mother as he takes a seat beside her. I can't help wondering if this meeting is bittersweet for him because of the loss of his mother.

"I've been looking forward to meeting you, Mrs. Snow." He then glances at my father. "And you as well, of course."

My father smiles as he lies back in his lounger. "I sure wish you had called before your visit so we could have made arrangements for your stay."

"I apologize for the surprise visit," Lance says, giving me a wink. "But I'm the kind of person who immediately acts when something is important to me."

My dad snorts, then grins looking in my direction when he tells Lance, "Well, I certainly can't fault you for that."

I give Lance a peck on the cheek and smile. "This was the best kind of surprise!"

My mother looks at the two of us for a moment before asking, "So, how long are you planning to visit, Lance?"

He turns to me. "A couple of days—unless Avery

would like me to stay longer."

I say nothing as I stare at him in wonder, still not quite convinced that Lance is really here sitting beside me.

"This occasion calls for refreshments!" my mom suddenly announces.

I offer to help and follow her into the kitchen, knowing she wants to talk. The moment we're alone, she says in a hushed voice, "Honey, he is even more handsome than you described."

I grin. "I know, but I didn't want you to think I was only interested in his looks."

My mother opens the fridge and starts taking out a variety of fruits and vegetables, along with various cheeses, meats, and crackers. Between the two of us, we create a simple but stylish charcuterie board in a matter of minutes.

It's kind of our thing for every game, and something the two of us take pride in.

"What are your plans while he's here?"

I laugh. "I haven't thought that far ahead. I'm still in a bit of shock."

"I can tell." She pauses for a moment, then asks in a concerned tone, "Are you happy to see him?"

Unable to contain it any longer, I confide in her. "I told him I loved him on the way here."

"Are you sure?" She grabs my hands and squeezes them tightly. "It's easy to get caught up in the excitement when someone surprises you like that."

I smile, deciding to be completely open with her. "I fell in love with Lance while I was in Crested Butte, and the feeling has only gotten stronger since."

My mother gives me a worried look. "But is he a good friend? That's more important because relationships can't survive without that."

"Lance is not only supportive, but he accepts me just as I am—panic attacks and all. That's why he came here to visit. He wants to find a way that we can be together." Tears spring to my eyes when I confess, "I can't tell you how much that means to me."

She nods, then gives me a tight squeeze. "I'm happy for you, honey."

It's not a surprise to me that she doesn't understand the kind of passionate love Lance and I share, since she's never experienced it herself. But my parents' loving friendship has always been an inspiration to me, and it's something I expect to build with Lance in the years to come.

She hands the finished platter to me. "Why don't you take this out to your handsome boyfriend while I get us some iced tea?"

As I walk out of the kitchen, I catch the two men having an intense conversation. Lance glances up and gives me a private smile before patting my dad on the back. "Sorry, Mr. Snow, it doesn't matter how bad their stats get, I'm a dedicated Bronco fan through and through."

My father tsks in mock disdain. "I'm afraid that's a mark against you in this family."

"Oh, Daddy! We're accepting of everyone in this family…including Bronco fans," I tease.

Setting down the charcuterie board, I admit to

Lance, "Personally, I just watch the game for the snacks."

Mom returns with the tea a few moments later. I sit back for the next few hours as my parents pepper Lance with questions about his family, details about his life in Crested Butte, and his experiences as a firefighter.

Throughout the afternoon game, my gaze keeps traveling back to Lance.

I sit there in pleasant silence, deeply touched by the lengths Lance is willing to go to be with me.

Candy for the Win

Lance

While I sit here talking to Avery's parents, I keep stealing glances at their daughter. She is absolutely irresistible with her twinkling blue eyes and kissable lips.

When Avery catches me lingering on those sexy lips of hers during the fourth quarter of the game, she gives me a coy smile. As soon as the Chiefs win, she suddenly stands up and announces that we need to be leaving.

I gladly take her lead and say goodbye to both of her parents. "Mrs. Snow, I'm glad to have finally met you."

"I feel the same. You're everything Avery said you were…" She then glances at her daughter with an amused smile. "…and more."

I turn to Mr. Snow next and shake his hand firmly. "It has been a pleasure to speak with you in person, sir."

"Agreed," he replies. "But please call me Joe. 'Sir' is reserved for refined individuals."

I find it humorous that his first and last name rhymes. Joe Snow is perfect for a bad pun, but I keep my smile to myself.

Avery's father turns to her and says in a serious tone, "I don't want you to come to work tomorrow. In fact, I'm taking over your shift for the next few days. Consider it paid leave."

Before Avery can respond, her mother raises her eyebrows. "It's never wise to go against management."

Avery laughs, then smiles at both of them. "I appreciate it."

Her father grins as he ushers her toward the front door and I hear him whisper, "It's good to see you smiling again, Pumpkin."

I notice a pink blush rising to Avery's cheeks as the two of us walk to her car. When she gives me a seductive smile, I am certain she's thinking what I'm thinking.

After making a quick trip back to the thrift shop to pick up Moonbeam and my luggage, Avery drives over to her apartment.

Once we get there, however, she insists I stand outside while she picks up the place.

"I don't care what it looks like," I call out to her, feeling foolish as I stand on the landing.

I nod and smile awkwardly at a neighbor. She eyes me suspiciously as she walks past.

Avery rips the door open and hands me Moonbeam. "She can keep you company while I make my place cat friendly."

The bewildered kitten squirms in my arms as I gaze out at the flat expanse that makes up Wichita. Although there are plenty of tall apartment buildings in the area, I miss the majestic presence of Crested Butte. The landscape here feels way too open and makes me slightly uncomfortable.

When I feel Moonbeam's tail twitching, I scratch her head and mutter to myself, "Don't worry, we'll get used to it."

Thankfully, Avery makes speedy work of cat-proofing the apartment and opens her door, inviting me inside with a playful smile.

The first thing I notice is her floor-to-ceiling row of bookcases that cover an entire wall. They are literally *stuffed* with books.

I chuckle. "I see you have your own library."

She gazes at her book collection with obvious pride. "Books let you live a thousand lives, you know."

I nod, finding her passion for them endearing.

Avery doesn't waste any time. As soon as I set Moonbeam down to the floor to explore, she grabs my hand and leads me straight to her bedroom. "Wanna check out my clean sheets?"

I smirk as I stare at her perfectly made bed. Placing my hands around her waist, I pull her close to me. "I'd be happy to make love to you on a pile of dirt. Really doesn't matter to me."

"Well, it matters to *me!*" Avery laughs, but her laughter soon quiets when we start to kiss. Desperate for one another, we quickly start stripping off our clothes. There is no denying the intense chemistry between the two of us, or our driving need to connect after being apart for so long.

"Give me a second," I murmur, pulling away from her for a moment. "There was something you left behind at the cabin." I grab my pants and pull a small cellophane package from my pocket.

I hold it up to her and smile. "The prize you won with your impressive dart-throwing skills."

She grins. "My candy necklace!"

"I found it under the nightstand when I was cleaning the cabin." I open the package and slip it over her head, adjusting the row of circular candy beads around her neck.

Avery smiles as runs her hands over the brightly colored pieces. "You're so sweet to bring it."

"I have special plans for this necklace," I murmur, getting hard just thinking about it.

Once she is free of her clothes, I hold out my arms to her and watch in silent admiration as this gorgeous woman walks into my embrace. Wrapping my arms around her naked body, I revel in the feel of her bare skin against mine.

My need for her won't be denied, so I gently coax her onto the bed. I lay on top of her body, propping myself up so I can stare at her freely.

Avery's strawberry blonde hair perfectly frames her exquisite face. I kiss her freckled nose before staring at the candy beads around her throat. "I've been imagining what I would do with this necklace for a while now."

Her eyes widen. "I can't imagine what that is."

"Let me show you…" I growl seductively. I lean down, resting my hard shaft against her pussy. Using my mouth, I gently separate one piece of the candy. The intimate contact is enhanced by the grazing of my teeth against her throat.

I wait a brief moment to build up her anticipation before biting down on the hard candy. When it breaks in my mouth, Avery lets out an excited squeak.

I pull back and smile at her. "Did you enjoy that?"

Avery's eyes flash with excitement. "When you bit down, it sent erotic shockwaves through my whole body." Wiggling her hips beneath me, she begs, "Do it again!"

"As you wish." I pause for a moment to slip on a condom. Singling out another piece of candy with my teeth, I purposely time it so that as I bite down to break the candy, my cock penetrates her wet pussy.

She purrs, her eyes luminous with desire. "I swear I almost climaxed just now. I had no idea a candy necklace could be an aphrodisiac…"

I chuckle, pressing my shaft deeper into her, captivated by her tight warmth. Staring into her eyes, I begin to slowly stroke her pussy as I continue to nibble her neck.

Avery grabs my ass in response, grinding herself against me. I take my time making love to her, expressing the depth of my feelings with every kiss, lick, and thrust.

Far into the night, the two of us indulge our carnal need for each other, basking in the intimate connection only lovers share.

Afterward, as we lay side by side on Avery's small bed, Moonbeam startles us by jumping up to join us. Avery laughs as she quickly covers us up with a sheet. "I completely forgot she was here."

"I guess she finished exploring the rest of your apartment," I chuckle as I watch the kitten walk to the head of the bed. She chooses to settle on Avery's chest, where she curls up and proceeds to purr.

I snicker. "Seems like she's making herself right at home."

Avery turns her head to stare at me.

"What?" I laugh, sensing she wants to say something.

When I see her worried expression, I tense a little.

"Lance…"

Bracing myself for the worst, I ask, "What is it, Avery?"

She bites her bottom lip, looking extremely nervous. "I can't express how much I appreciate that you are willing to move to Wichita."

"But?" My hope starts to fade as I wait for the ax to fall.

She gives me a guilty smile.

Although I thought I was prepared for anything, she completely surprises me when she says, "I think I'd rather live in Crested Butte."

I stare at her in shock—just before I burst out laughing with relief.

Forever Mine

Avery

Lance shakes his head in disbelief. "Do you mind explaining what you mean by that?"

Knowing I've just stunned him with my confession, I explain, "I've been doing a lot of research lately."

"Go on," he encourages.

I start petting Moonbeam when I tell him, "I was surprised to discover that small towns are safer for firefighters than bigger cities. The crews go on fewer emergency calls during the year, and a smaller percentage of those calls actually involve fires."

I nod. "I can verify that."

"Of course, there are the wildfires in Crested Butte which we don't have here in Wichita. However, I've been researching that as well. Based on what I found, the chances of a firefighter perishing in a wildfire are about half that of structural fires. I was also shocked to learn that as an occupation, roofers and delivery drivers are more likely to die on the job than firefighters."

I look at Lance apologetically. "I know this probably sounds gruesome since we are talking about deaths on a job, but knowing all of this has helped me."

He looks at me thoughtfully. "I understand."

"Learning all this has made me think and I realize that if you had told me you were a delivery driver, I wouldn't have batted an eye. So, having this information gives me a healthier perspective about your job. If I were to choose where you worked, I would always pick a small town over a big city because it would be safer."

Lance nods with tenderness in his eyes.

I feel a blush rise to my cheeks when I confess, "But it's not just you that I'm thinking of by choosing Crested Butte. There also happens to be a library I've fallen in love with."

"Should I be jealous of Old Rock?" he chuckles, leaning in close to kiss me on the lips before giving Moonbeam a chin scratch.

"There's no need…I love you both equally," I tease. Gazing up at the ceiling, I let out a contented sigh. "Truly, it's the best kind of threesome I could imagine."

"Hmm…I never realized you were into that," Lance states with a wicked grin as he moves Moonbeam off the bed before tickling me mercilessly.

After calling Mr. Gregory to confirm that the position is still available, Lance helps me pack up my apartment in boxes. Although it is bittersweet to be leaving my family and the place of my birth, with every box I tape up, I hear the quote by Jack London, "Deep in the forest a call was sounding…"

I know with certainty that this is the path I am meant to take, and for the first time in a long time, I feel no fear about my future.

With Ladybug packed to the gills and the rest of my things set to arrive in two weeks, I wave to my family as I ready myself to begin this new journey with Lance.

However, just before I'm about to head out, Jake comes up to the car and hands me a gift bag.

"What this?" I ask, smiling at him.

Jake's face turns beat red. "Remember when I said that you inspire me?"

I nod as I remove the copious amounts of tissue paper from the bag, laughing as I hand them all back to Jake. My laughter stops when I lift out a beautiful vase. It's covered in a mosaic pattern of small glass pieces, creating a charming mountain scene. I immediately recognize the iconic peak and grin at him.

"It's Crested Butte!"

He nods, looking pleased.

"This is so beautiful, Jake. I can't imagine how much this must have cost you."

His face grows even redder when he tells me. "It didn't cost me a thing, sis."

I look at him in wonder. "You made this?" I turn the vase slowly in my hands to admire it.

Jake laughs, looking exceedingly self-conscious. "I've been collecting all of the broken glass items we receive at the thrift shop with the intention of repurposing them." He stares at the vase with obvious pride. "This is my very first creation, and it was inspired by you. I started working on it while you were in Colorado."

"You should keep this because it's your first," I insist, trying to hand it back to him.

He holds his hands up and refuses to take it. "No, it's yours. I thought of you and your badassery with every glass piece I added to it."

Jake then looks at me tenderly, tears glistening in his eyes. "I'm proud of you, sis."

Struggling not to cry myself, my voice trembles when I tell him, "I'm going to miss you, Jake."

He nods. "I plan to come out to visit so I see this library of yours."

"'Kay…" I choke out.

Lance takes the vase from me and gently wraps it in his jacket, setting it in a safe place in the back of the car.

Jake stands on the curb with my parents and they wave as I drive off.

"Keep up the badassery, sis!"

I laugh through my tears as I stick my arm out the window and wave back at them.

Even though I hate the idea of leaving my family behind, I'm strengthened by their support and I am bursting with a quiet confidence knowing I'm now Old Rock's official librarian.

I smile at Lance, who has Moonbeam on his lap. With a sense of wonder and disbelief, I declare, "We're doing this!"

He nods, stating with conviction, "Yes, we are."

I take a shorter route on the back roads that take me through Pueblo, so I can skip the gridlock of Denver altogether. Passing through many small towns on the plains along the way, I catch my breath when I finally spot the faint blue outline of the Rocky Mountains in the far distance.

Rather than fear them, I'm overcome with the thrill of adventure.

I feel like a kid again.

Hours later, when I reach the steep road up the first mountain peak, my hands start to get clammy. Despite my gum, essential oils, and affirmations, I begin to feel the familiar pressure in my chest and glance at Lance in concern.

He smiles, his eyes full of compassion. "Something ingrained since childhood isn't going to be solved overnight, my love."

My heart skips a beat when he calls me "my love" and I struggle to hear the words he says after, only catching the last part.

"…take over driving."

I'm embarrassed having to ask him to repeat himself, but he seems amused.

"I asked if you would like me to drive the final leg. If you sit in the passenger seat with Moonbeam, she'll help keep you calm so you can enjoy the beautiful scenery— not just survive it."

Touched by his thoughtful offer, I pull over to the side of the road and we make the switch. The moment I buckle myself in and place Moonbeam on my lap, I feel more at ease. I look at Lance and smile. "Thank you."

"My pleasure." When he winks at me, I fall even more in love with the man.

As Lance continues driving the steep road up the mountain, I realize that the steps I've taken to conquer my fears have helped to temper my phobic fear of heights.

For the first time in my life, I become enchanted by the beauty of the rugged, snow-covered peaks as we climb higher and higher. The pristine white of the freshly fallen snow covering the trees gives the entire landscape a fairy-tale-like quality.

When we finally crest the last peak, I hold my breath as we begin the downward journey into the town of Crested Butte. It feels wonderfully surreal to be here again…

My heart begins to race as I pet Moonbeam. It is not out of fear, but affection for this place. When Lance slows down as we pass over a cattle grate, I grin.

"You don't get those in Wichita."

Sitting back in my seat, I gaze at the towering peak of Crested Butte. I remember how that tall mountain once terrified me, but now it brings me a unique sense of peace.

Home…

I adjust Moonbeam on my lap and lean in, so I can kiss Lance on the cheek. "Are you happy to be back home?"

He smirks. "I already told you where my home is."

I wink at him, loving his answer.

Tears prick my eyes as pleasant memories flood over me as we drive past Bram's diner, Annie's Home

Cookin'. Lance then turns down the town's main street.

Elk Avenue is covered in freshly fallen snow, and I notice that all of the shops are decorated for the holidays. I smile to myself, excited by the prospect of making new memories here with Lance.

I'm surprised when he makes an unexpected detour and passes by the fire station. Remembering his punishment for bringing the kitten to the station, I ask, "Are you still scrubbing the bathrooms?"

"Of course," Lance replies. "Chief Higgins isn't about to let Montoya and me off."

I chuckle as I pet Moonbeam. "At least the Chief is consistent."

"That's certainly one word for him," he laughs. As we continue down the street, Lance says, "Well, well…would you look at that?"

I suck in a quick breath when I look up to see Old Rock.

It wasn't that long ago that I was unsure if I would ever see the library again. As I stare at the stone building, I have no doubt that this is exactly where I am meant to be.

"Would you like to go inside?" Lance asks.

Thrilled by the suggestion, I answer enthusiastically, "I'd love to."

Lance finds a spot in the small parking lot and turns off the engine. He lets out a nervous sigh as he reaches back to grab his jacket.

"Is everything okay?" I ask.

He nods, then carefully unwraps the vase before slipping his jacket on. He then helps me place Moonbeam into her carrier and suggests, "Why don't we bring her?"

"Only service animals are allowed…" I tell him. However, I really hate the thought of leaving her alone in the car after the long drive.

Lance snorts. "What's the worst that can happen? You scrub the library toilets for a year?"

I laugh. "I suppose that would only be fair."

I take his hand, and he helps me out of the car. As we walk up to the entrance, I notice Mr. Zeigler standing near the entrance. He breaks into a toothy grin and immediately pulls off his cap. "Miss Snow! What a pleasant surprise to see you again."

"It's lovely to see you, too," I answer, tickled to see him.

Switching the cat carrier to my other hand, I shake the hand he offers me. But I can't help blushing slightly when I think back on the candy necklace I won at his booth.

"Please, go before me," Mr. Zeigler insists, opening the door for us.

The moment I step inside, I let out a surprised gasp. The first floor has been decorated with purple and gold balloons, along with silver streamers that have been artfully strung from the ceiling.

I squeeze Lance's arm. "It looks so pretty!"

I notice Flora Elwood on the other side of the empty library. The moment she sees me, she waves enthusiastically. "Welcome back, Miss Snow."

I suddenly wonder if she put up decorations to welcome me as the new librarian.

Lance places his hand on the small of my back as we walk over to greet her, but he abruptly stops when we reach the center of the room. Turning to face me, he takes the cat carrier from my hand and gently sets Moonbeam on the floor.

Then he reaches into his jacket. I watch in stunned silence as Lance slowly gets down on one knee and looks up at me with a charming smile.

I hold my breath when he opens the velvet box and holds up a diamond ring. At the same time, people start streaming down the stairs from the upper level.

Time stands still as I look into his loving eyes.

"Avery Snow, we've returned to Crested Butte to start a life together. I want to make it official, so I'm here before you on bended knee to declare my love and to announce to the world that I want to spend the rest of my life with you."

Lance looks up at me and smiles. "Will you marry me?"

Touched by his romantic proposal, I hold out my trembling hand. "I would be honored to be your wife."

"What was that? We couldn't hear it in the back!" I hear Gavin shout.

I look up to see all four of his brothers standing in a line. Grinning, I answer so *everyone* can hear. "I said yes!"

The whole library breaks out in applause as Lance slips the ring onto my finger and stands up to give me a long, passionate kiss.

We break from our tender embrace amid a chorus of hoots and hollers from the crowd. I scan the room, touched to see that both Leith and Clara are in attendance.

"Forever has a nice *ring* to it, doesn't it, lass?" Clara calls out to me.

I laugh as I hold up my hand and nod to her.

Davy, the older man who gave Lance his seat at the diner for our "pseudo date," shouts from the back, "What are the older Macallan boys gonna do now that their baby brother is 'bout to beat them to the altar?"

"It sucks to be them," Lance answers, giving me another kiss. "Because I've got this beautiful librarian all to myself."

I can't stop smiling. I could never imagine a proposal as perfect as this. Here I am, a bona fide book lover, and I just had the man of my dreams propose to me in this beautiful old library, surrounded by books and a room full of smiling faces—with a fluffy white kitten to boot.

Bursting with love for Lance, I wrap my arms around him and stand on tiptoes to give him a kiss. "I don't think I could love you any more than I do right now, Lance Macallan."

Later that evening, still flying on the high of our engagement, Lance takes me back to the old bench on his family's property. Brushing off the newly fallen snow, he gestures to me to sit and takes a seat beside me.

As the two of us look out over the snowy field where the old Macallan house once stood, he takes my mittened hand in his. "I wanted to come here tonight because something important happened recently."

I turn my head to meet his gaze and he smiles at me. "The nightmares have stopped."

I open my mouth in surprise. "That's incredible, Lance!"

He nods, then glances back at the field.

In a solemn tone, he tells me, "Ever since I was a wee *bairn*, I've believed I was destined to die in the flames like my mother. But I understand now that she sacrificed her life so I would be free from that fate."

Lance looks at me, brimming with confidence. "I know with certainty that my mother is smiling down on us."

"Yes…" Tears fill my eyes because, like him, I can feel her warm spirit here with us.

Lance furrows his brow. "It's strange…" He looks back out on the field covered in white. "All of my life, I have come to this place and been strangled with guilt. But now I feel at peace here."

"It is peaceful," I agree breathlessly.

I can't stop smiling as I sit in comfortable silence on the cold bench with my fiancé, my heart bursting with hope for the future.

I came to Crested Butte grudgingly, never imagining that I would find my happy-ever-after here…

"Avery, there's one more place I'd like to take you before the sun goes down." I stand up and eagerly take the hand he holds out to me. Leading me to his truck, he explains, "We'll need to drive for this one."

I'm grateful to escape back into the warmth of the truck. I place my hands near the heater as he takes me on a back road that follows the expansive length of his father's property.

I smile when he finally stops at a scenic hill lined with trees. We both stare through the windshield as the sun begins setting behind the peak.

It's here that Lance tells me, "My parents had a plan when they bought their land. The two of them wanted to leave a legacy for future generations. To do that, they divided this property into five parcels so that as each child marries, they could claim a portion of it."

Lance's eyes flash with excitement. "What you're looking at is the spot of our future home."

My jaw drops. I know that land in Crested Butte is scarce, and I never dreamed we could own land as picturesque as this. "I can't believe it!"

He states proudly, "I naturally get first choice as the first in the family to marry."

Overcome with emotion, I clasp his hand. "It's like we're following in your parents' footsteps—starting a brand-new life together as we build it from the ground up."

"Exactly," he agrees, hugging me tightly. "Starting in late spring, I'm leaving my job at the motel—with my gran's blessing. My plan is to devote those days to building a home we can be proud of."

Energized by the idea of literally building our future together, I give him an impassioned kiss. Looking back at the empty field, I tell him with excitement, "I'll be out here on my days off so we can build it together."

Pulling me into his lap, Lance wraps me in his warm embrace as we both stare at the beginning of our journey as a couple. I can already envision our little house with the majestic peak towering behind it.

I smile in wonder as I gaze into Lance's eyes.

This is what forever looks like...

Reviews mean the world to me, my friend 🩶
I truly appreciate you taking the time to review.
Meeting My Forever!

Get ready for Malcolm's story next!

Want more

Lance and Avery?

I have a special scene I've written just for you! Join Avery and Lance as they plan their upcoming wedding and share some "alone time" outdoors (wink, wink).

Go here (bookhip.com/DFLRSBT) to subscribe to my mailing list to read this swoony peek into their future.

(or use the QR code below)

****If you are already signed up, click on the same link to read it!***

COMING NEXT

*The next book in The Brother's Macallan series is coming!

Meeting My Honeybun

The Macallan Brothers Book 2

Available for Purchase

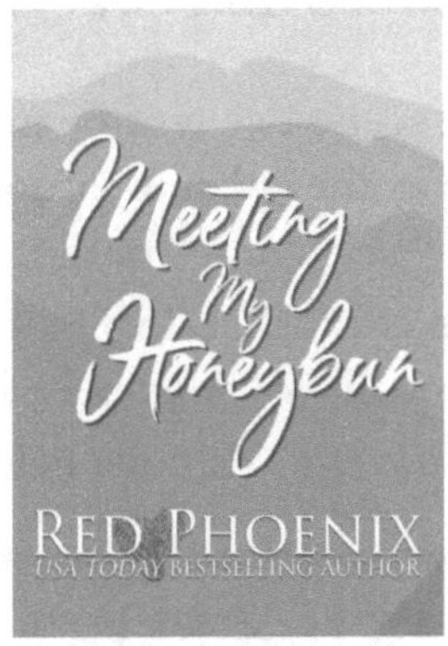

Malcolm Macallan – the hardworking, no-nonsense President of the credit union in the mountain town of Crested Butte is a secret romantic who writes poetry nobody reads.

He doesn't know it yet, but he has caught the eye of the mysterious new baker, a single mom with a hidden past and a ball-loving Golden Retriever.

Find out what happens when a serious Banker and a talented Baker collide over cake…

Want to hang with my friends?

Hey Everyone!

I'm Red Phoenix, a proud Indie Author who follows her muses with a passion. Over the years, my fans have become like family.

When I'm not writing, you can find me online with readers.

I heart my fans! ~Red

To find out more visit my Website
redphoenixauthor.com
Follow Me on BookBub
bookbub.com/authors/red-phoenix
Newsletter: Sign up
redphoenixauthor.com/newsletter-signup
Facebook: AuthorRedPhoenix
Twitter: @redphoenix69
Instagram: RedPhoenixAuthor
I invite you to join my reader Group!
facebook.com/groups/539875076052037

SIGN UP FOR MY NEWSLETTER
HERE FOR THE LATEST RED
PHOENIX UPDATES

FOLLOW ME ON INSTAGRAM
INSTAGRAM.COM/REDPHOENIXAUTHOR

SALES, GIVEAWAYS, NEW
RELEASES, PREORDER LINKS,
AND MORE!

SIGN UP HERE
REDPHOENIXAUTHOR.COM/NEWSLETTER-
SIGNUP